MUTE WITNESS

I had detected no sound or movement, but her eyes
were open and, as I approached, she fixed them on me
with an agonised stare. There were two bedside tables and
on the one on her right, where I was standing, were a
carafe of water, two tumblers, some bottles of pills and
medicine and a jotting pad, with a felt pen attached to it
by a cord. Although wavering and unsteady, Edna's hand
left me in small doubt as to which of these objects it was
seeking and I took up the pad, placed it on the sheet in
front of her, and fitted the pen between thumb and forefinger. Her eyes followed my every movement and before
she began to write they met mine in a final anguished look
of appeal.

There appeared to be three separate words on the slip
of paper, one below the other and although I stared at
them with all the concentration I could muster I got no
further than admitting that the first and third were illegible, while the second, if it was a word, made no sense at
all. They looked like this:

Agatha Christie

DEATH ON THE NILE
A HOLIDAY FOR MURDER
THE MOUSETRAP AND
  OTHER PLAYS
THE MYSTERIOUS AFFAIR AT
  STYLES
POIROT INVESTIGATES
POSTERN OF FATE
THE SECRET ADVERSARY
THE SEVEN DIALS MYSTERY
SLEEPING MURDER

Patricia Wentworth

THE FINGERPRINT
THE IVORY DAGGER
THE LISTENING EYE
MISS SILVER COMES TO STAY
POISON IN THE PEN
SHE CAME BACK

Margery Allingham

BLACK PLUMES
DANCERS IN MOURNING
FLOWERS FOR THE JUDGE
PEARLS BEFORE SWINE
THE TIGER IN THE SMOKE

Dorothy Simpson

THE NIGHT SHE DIED
SIX FEET UNDER

John Greenwood

MOSLEY BY MOONLIGHT
MURDER, MR. MOSLEY

Catherine Aird

HENRIETTA WHO
LAST RESPECTS
A MOST CONTAGIOUS GAME
PARTING BREATH
SLIGHT MOURNING
SOME DIE ELOQUENT

Elizabeth Daly

AND DANGEROUS TO KNOW
THE BOOK OF THE LION
HOUSE WITHOUT THE DOOR
NOTHING CAN RESCUE ME
SOMEWHERE IN THE HOUSE
THROUGH THE WALL
UNEXPECTED NIGHT

Jonathan Ross

DIMINISHED BY DEATH

Anne Morice

MURDER IN OUTLINE
MURDER POST-DATED
SCARED TO DEATH

Scared to Death

Anne Morice

BANTAM BOOKS

TORONTO · NEW YORK · LONDON · SYDNEY · AUCKLAND

*This low-priced Bantam Book
has been completely reset in a type face
designed for easy reading, and was printed
from new plates. It contains the complete
text of the original hard-cover edition.*
NOT ONE WORD HAS BEEN OMITTED.

SCARED TO DEATH

*A Bantam Book / published by arrangement with
St. Martin's Press*

PRINTING HISTORY
*St. Martin's edition published January 1979
Bantam edition / May 1986*

ISBN 0-553-25628-9

Published simultaneously in the United States and Canada

PRINTED IN THE UNITED STATES OF AMERICA

O   0 9 8 7 6 5 4 3 2 1

Scared to Death

CHAPTER ONE

•

"You sit in front with me, Tessa," Vi said in her masterful way, having announced her arrival at my cousin Toby's house with a fanfare of blasts on the horn. "Marge needs the whole of the back seat to spread out her racing pages and *The Sporting Life*," she explained, although I was aware, having accompanied them to race meetings in the past that the back seat also provided a distinctly more advantageous position when the picnic basket came out.

Vi and Marge were sisters, both now middle-aged, but handsome, tall and vigorous, one of whom had been married and the other not and Vi, the unmarried one, was conspicuously more masterful than Marge. Two recent deaths, that of their mother and Marge's husband, had released them from separate lives of tyranny and they now lived together in opulent and merry style in a pretty house about two miles from the riverside town of Storhampton, and indulged their masterful natures and capacity for enjoyment to the full by organising jumble sales, coffee mornings and wine and cheese parties galore. Apart from this and the keen interest they took in all their neighbours' affairs, their principal passions in life centred on racing and the theatre.

"And if anyone asks you," Vi continued, "remember to say that Toby had intended to come with us, but changed his mind at the last minute."

"If anyone asks me what?" I enquired, thinking that this

unknown questioner would need to have dropped in from another planet that very morning if he could seriously believe that my cousin Toby would have contemplated accompanying us on such a jaunt for a single moment. Race meetings are notorious for so many of the features of life which he is most keen to avoid, including cruel exposure to the elements, a great deal of walking about, a terrible crush of people, some of them shouting and, above all, horses.

"If anyone asks where he is," Vi explained with studied patience, "tiresome old Edna Mortimer was trying to scrounge a lift and I had to choke her off somehow. Apart from being such a bore, it was only a ruse to save her own petrol. I didn't exactly lie about it, but I let it be understood that Toby was coming with us and there wouldn't be room for her."

Passing over the fact that it must have required some ingenuity to let such a thing as that be understood without exactly lying about it, I promised not to forget.

"There really isn't room for her, even without Toby," Marge explained, which a glance at the back seat confirmed. "Not even for her fur coat, without her inside it."

"You had better say he wasn't feeling well," Vi advised, spelling it out for me, as she was so apt to do. "That would be quite in character for Toby."

"Might it not sound even better," I suggested, "to say that he's had to go to Storhampton to help with organising the Festival?"

"My dear child, we all know that Edna is stupid, ignorant and self-centred, but even she would be aware that the Festival has been cancelled."

These masterful ladies sometimes positively ask for a squashing and I could not resist it.

"Stupid, ignorant and out of date too. The Festival is on again."

Her grip on the wheel did not falter, but I could tell that I had pierced her defences and Marge was so far diverted from her study of the racing pages as to let out a high scream of excitement:

"On again? Since when, Tessa?"

"Last night. Underground negotiations have been going on for several days, but last night clinched it. Our angel fairy godfather has stepped into the breach in the nick of time."

"And put up some money?"

"Good as. Not actual cash, but a guarantee against losses of up to five thousand. Since he'll inevitably be required to stump up every penny, it amounts to the same thing."

"What's the name of this madman?" Vi demanded.

"David Winter, which is probably one you've come across in a long life of theatre going. And he's no madman. One condition of this guarantee is an option on each of the plays. Since there are three of them, all getting their first airing and all by fairly successful authors, it would be funny if there wasn't at least one winner in the bunch. Five thousand isn't an awful lot to pay for the rights, quite apart from all the wonderful publicity he'll get as our Saviour of the Arts."

"And Toby was the one to bring off this coup?"

"He had a hand in it. Having flogged himself into a jelly to turn out a play specially for the occasion, he was understandably reluctant to see it buried and forgotten. I have to confess that his interest in the Festival in general doesn't go very deep."

"But, presumably, if his play is any good, this David Winter would have put it on anyway?"

"Oh, very likely, but you know how they always grab at the chance to try things out on audiences in a modest way before taking the big plunge? By the time this one gets to London, if it does, it will probably have been completely re-written, according to where the Storhampton laughs came. By the way, what makes you think Mrs. Mortimer would be wearing a fur coat on this mild May morning?"

"She always goes racing in mink," Vi replied. "It has nothing to do with the seasons. She's like Toby and his play; she enjoys parading her possessions in front of an audience."

"There's a horse called Festive Lad in the two o'clock," Marge informed us. "It's got no form, but perhaps we should put something on?"

The curious thing about Marge's betting system was that despite her keen and well informed study of the subject, which embraced such esoteric points as the antecedents and past performance of every horse in the race, whether it preferred soft going to hard, five furlongs to a mile and how favourable or otherwise the draw, yet when it came to slapping down her money she invariably backed the runner whose name provided some such loose connection as this. Weirder still was the fact that it invariably paid off. I suggested that if it did so this time she should put her winnings into the fund for the Storhampton Music and Drama Festival.

"Oh, we've already done our bit there," she assured me. "In fact, Vi and I raised over fifty pounds at a Cheese and Wine. Edna's the one you ought to be after for a contribution. And I wish you luck!"

"Oh, I know, she's a hopeless case. Helena Plowman, who's the Treasurer, is simply furious with her. She sent out an appeal to all the prominent citizens and Edna was the only one who didn't stump up a cent. The most sickening thing of all was that she made poor old Tilly write back a very sanctimonious letter saying that, with so much distress and poverty in the world, she preferred to send whatever she could afford to more deserving charities."

"She has a point there," Vi suggested.

"Oh, you bet, but from what I hear of Edna Mortimer, her contributions to the deserving charities wouldn't cover a postage stamp. And she evidently can't bring herself to part with any of her minks."

"Now, you mustn't get bitter about it, Tessa! We all know you have this Festival very much at heart, but carping doesn't suit you, and Edna certainly isn't worth it. She's a silly, stuck-up, vain old woman, but quite unimportant."

As comments went, this proved to be fairly wide of the mark and the one which followed from the back seat was a lot more constructive.

"There's a horse called Bitter Aloes in the three-thirty," Marge announced. "Never done the distance, but I think Tessa should back it, I honestly do."

CHAPTER TWO

•

Edna Mortimer, immediately recognisable from the back of her portly form by the massive ankle-length mink and hideous green velvet turban, was just in front of me in the paying out queue. When she turned sideways to stuff a bundle of notes furtively into her crocodile bag, it was apparent that all this finery was proving a little too much for her on such a warm afternoon, although the purple flush and beads of sweat may have owed something to the triumph of watching Bitter Aloes come streaking in ahead of the field, at thirty-three to one.

"You were on it too, were you, Mrs. Mortimer?" I asked, catching her up as she plodded rather unsteadily towards the Members' Enclosure.

"Only a flutter," she said defensively. "I make it a rule never to stake more than a pound. Can't imagine why they had to put the minimum up to fifty pence. Thirty each way suited me well enough."

"Still, pretty good price, wasn't it? Did you back it on a hunch?"

"No, through my grand-daughter's fiancé. He's a great friend of the trainer. Not that my family bothers to pass on information of that kind and Camilla's the worst of the lot, as a rule, but she did happen to mention it this morning. Probably thought I wasn't listening."

We had entered the enclosure by this time and the first batch of riders for the next race was cantering past on

their way to the start. On our left, the stands were already
jammed with spectators, for this was the big event of the
day, with Vi and Marge, field glasses at the ready, no
doubt somewhere in the thick of it all, but it was impossible to pick them out.

Most of the wooden seats on the grass slope in front
were also occupied by two or more people, but there was
one, right out on its own, within yards of the rails and
almost level with the finishing post, which for some reason
had been neglected by everyone. Edna noticed it in a
flash and lumbered towards it, evidently bent on getting
possession before some rival claimant materialised. Having nowhere in particular to go, I followed her.

"What are you on this time?" I asked, striving to hit a
chatty note, for in fact her appearance made me a little
uneasy. The flush had deepened, if anything, and she was
now mopping her forehead with a handkerchief.

The question prompted another resentful look from her
watery pale blue eyes, but she was spared the necessity of
telling me to mind my own business, and incidentally of
asking where Toby was, by the fact that the unseen commentator on the roof had begun to bellow out names and
colours of the runners. He did this in a very practised and
professional way, which was just as well because we should
have had almost as good a view of the race if we had been
sitting in the next county. In the last few seconds, when
his voice was drowned in the roars and exhortations of the
crowd, we got a streaking glimpse of half a dozen jockey
caps and then it was all over, explaining conclusively why
the front bench had been ours for the taking.

I waited till the numbers went up, then read them out
to Edna, but she made no response and gave no indication
of intending to move, so I left her and went in search of
my hostesses.

I found them in the paddock, marking their race cards
with rings and crosses, as Marge called out knowledgeable
comments about the horses on parade. She did this with
so much authority and unself-conscious clarity of tone that
I felt sure her remarks must be influencing countless
spectators around her, who would discard their previous

opinions forthwith and hurry off to follow her advice, quite unaware that when her turn came she was infinitely more likely to back the one whose name reminded her of a tabby cat she had known and loved as a child.

There was a ferrety looking young man standing between them, wearing a brown trilby hat a size too large, which he doffed when Vi introduced us and in doing so revealed himself to be an inch shorter than either of his companions.

"This is Bernard Plowman, Tessa, Camilla's young man," she said, giving me a smart rap on the arm, presumably as a reminder that Toby had intended to come with us, but had changed his mind at the last minute. "I don't think you two have met, have you? This is Tessa Price, Bernard, who is Toby Crichton's cousin and, whatever you've been up to, you'd better keep it dark because her husband is a policeman."

"Oh really?" he muttered, glancing nervously around, as though expecting to spot a helmet somewhere in the crowd.

"He's not here, though," I explained. "He was hoping to come with us, but he got caught up with some criminals at the last minute."

This flippancy earned me a scowl of disapproval from Vi, while Marge announced firmly:

"I must say, I fancy number eleven. He's got a good back. Looks like a stayer. Wonder how much weight he's carrying?"

"Funny sort of movement, though," Vi said, keeping her end up. "You'd think he had corns."

Whereupon, without another word and as though obeying some private summons from the Great Steward in the Sky, they both tucked their ballpoints into their bags and plunged away in the direction of the Tote.

Several other people around us immediately followed suit, leaving me and Bernard temporarily isolated, leaning on the rail and watching the jockeys mount.

"I've just been talking to Camilla's grandmother," I told him.

"Step, if you don't mind!"

"I don't mind at all, except that step-grandmother does make rather a mouthful. You'll be interested to hear that you're in high favour."

"Me? That'll be the day!"

"I think she cleaned up quite a bit from that tip of yours in the third race."

He shook his head, looked both puzzled and faintly uneasy.

"Not me, lady. I never gave anyone a tip in my life."

"You've not heard of a horse called Bitter Aloes? I understood the trainer was a friend of yours?"

"Sorry," he said with a tightlipped smile, "I don't know any trainers. My mother has a few friends in that world, but this is the first time I've been on a race course since I was dragged to the Derby at the age of fourteen; and I don't much care if I never see another one."

"Why are you here to-day, then?"

"Usual reason. Step-gran had a whim to come, but couldn't manage on her own, so Camilla jumped in and told her we were going anyway and she could come with us. My God, she even insisted on lumbering me with this ghastly hat, which belonged to her father or something," he said disgustedly, raising his right hand to push the offending hat further back on his head, where it looked more ridiculous than ever, and I noticed that he was wearing a flashy and expensive looking gold watch, with a brilliant sapphire blue face, which told me something else about him. I enjoy collecting such small and seemingly trivial insights; they rarely prove rewarding in themselves, but I regard the exercise as good practice and a way of keeping my hand in.

"What's so special about wearing a hat?" I enquired.

"God knows. I suppose Camilla was afraid the old tartar would turn up her nose at a bareheaded member of the hoi polloi. I feel like a perfect Charlie, I don't mind telling you. In fact this would be a good moment to go and lose it in the Gents, while I've got the chance."

"Where is Camilla?" I asked, as we walked away.

"Oh, somewhere around. She keeps bumping into peo-ple she knows, so I expect she's having a nip with some of them. It's the social side which mainly appeals to her, as you can probably imagine."

I responded to this with a non-committal nod and then, having no winnings to collect from the last race and no inspiration for the next one, made a fanning out movement and entered the peaceful caverns of the Ladies Cloakroom. Bernard's remark had given me the idea of dispensing with my coat, though remembering to draw a large cross on the last page of my race card as a reminder to retrieve it again before we left.

I noticed, while waiting at the counter for my ticket, that a lot of other women had had the same idea and there was a rackful of coats and macintoshes stretching right back to the wall. Some had even discarded their hats and there were about half a dozen of these on a shelf above, one of them, I was interested to see, being a squashy green velvet turban, suggesting that Edna too had succumbed and divested herself of some of the trappings of grandeur.

This was not so, however, for when I rejoined Vi and Marge for the last race we were able to find three places in the centre of the stand and, looking down on the scene below, I saw Edna, still fully clothed and back on her lonely bench out in front. So a possible answer was that some other woman, mortified at finding herself wearing the identical hat, had bundled it out of sight with all speed. I was about to pass on these conjectures to Marge, who might have appreciated them, but at this moment the off was announced on the loud speaker and we stood up as one man and peered into the distant view, while the crowd below us started moving down towards the rails. It was not until it was all over and the ground was emptying again that I noticed that Edna still made no movement, but remained seated in her isolation, like a sagging, fur covered Rock of Gibraltar.

CHAPTER THREE

•

The journey ended with lovers meeting in the car park, although neither of them looked particularly ecstatic. They were drooping over a small and shabby looking car, which was one of only half a dozen left by then, two minor hitches having delayed our own departure.

The first came about through Vi and Marge both having picked the last winner of the day, which unfortunately had been the favourite and had therefore been obliged to queue up behind at least twenty other people who were waiting for the pay-out. Having emerged, triumphant but apologetic from this ordeal, they gathered me up at the exit, where I had been waiting in a somewhat martyred attitude, at which point I tossed my race card into the litter bin and was simultaneously struck by a mental picture of the large cross on its end page. There followed a general reshuffle of the martyred and apologetic expressions and I cantered away to collect my coat.

It was remarkable, in view of the rapidly dispersing crowd, how many outer garments still languished in the cloakroom, but I concluded that there must be other people in the world just as forgetful as myself, among them, apparently, the owner of the green velvet turban, and I could not resist dallying still further, to ask the attendant whether many articles were left unclaimed for all time.

"More than you think," she replied, so she must have been a mind reader.

"Isn't that Camilla and Bernard over there?" Vi asked, unlocking her Rover. "They look stranded. Something gone wrong with the car, do you suppose?"

"I only got ninety pence on the last one," Marge said, pursuing her own train of thought. "I should have backed it for a win only. All the same, I reckon I'm about two pounds up on the day, which is pretty good going."

"Did you deduct the price of the drinks?" Vi asked.

"Certainly not, I count that as expenses."

"Well, I don't and I'm about two pounds down on the day, so that works out quite satisfactorily."

"And I've probably done better than either of you," I admitted. "What with good old Bitter Aloes and the fact that neither of you would have another drink."

"You can pay on the toll bridge going home; but it looks as though Bernard and Camilla are coming over, so we'd better wait and find out what's up. Anything wrong, Camilla?"

"Nothing serious, thanks, except that Bernard and I are stuck here, waiting for Edna. You wouldn't know where she's got to, I suppose?"

"Not a clue, I'm afraid."

"She probably had some winnings to collect and it always seems to take her longer than anyone else. She keeps dodging in and out of queues, whenever she sees a chance of getting ahead, and it never works."

"I do that in the Post Office," Marge admitted, "and it never works there either. I wonder why?"

Camilla did not offer any explanation, but smiled broadly, showing a lot of teeth and gums. She tended to do this rather indiscriminately, sometimes as a substitute for the spoken word, although whether from stupidity or indifference was uncertain.

She was a thin, vapid looking blonde, the same age as myself, whom I had known for years, without ever becoming close friends with, for we had been flung together willy nilly, when I was taken as a child to visit my cousin Toby at Roakes Common. Too many adults suffer from the illusion that a pair of children need only to have been born within months of each other to become inseparable friends on sight, which is certainly not a rule they would apply to their own contemporaries and, in the case of Camilla and myself, our age and sex were about the only two factors we had in common.

I feel sure the antipathy had been entirely mutual, but I still maintain that I had more excuse, for not only had she been orphaned at the age of six, which in those days I regarded as the most romantic and enviable state on earth, but she was also reputed to be sole heiress to her grandfather's vast fortune, which in some ways was even better. Moreover, she was sickeningly well behaved, clean and tidy and ingratiating to her elders.

These days, however, I was usually able to return her vacuous smile without rancour, for such qualities cease to be so despicable in one's twenties and furthermore the vast fortune had now passed into other hands. Benjamin Mortimer, the grandfather who had amassed it, had upset everyone's calculations by marrying a widow he had met on a Greek cruise and on his death, a year or two later, it was revealed that his entire property had been left to her, to dispose of as she saw fit. Unluckily for Camilla, disposing of it was the last thing she had in mind.

"Perhaps the system worked this time, though," Bernard said, reverting to the theme of the missing step-grandmother, "and she was in and out of there before anyone saw her. Probably counting up the loot in the Ladies Cloakroom."

Vi glanced at me enquiringly and I shook my head:

"No, she wasn't in there. I haven't seen her for at least half an hour."

"She can't have been taken ill or anything," Camilla said, striving, I imagine, to keep a note of disappointment out of her voice, "because they'd have taken her to the first-aid post and put out the news on the loud speaker by now. Oh well, I suppose she's met a friend or something."

There was a brief pause while the rest of us considered this improbable solution and then Camilla added:

"Well, no need to hold you lot up. Bernard and I will just have to stick it out until she elects to come."

"The only thing is," Bernard said hesitantly, "what about poor old Tilly?"

"I know, but it can't be helped."

"What has Tilly got to do with it?" Vi asked.

"Waiting for us at the roundabout," Bernard explained. "She's been shopping and what not, in the town, and we'd arranged to pick her up half an hour after the last race, so we're running late already."

The poor old Tilly thus referred to was Matilda Prettyman, who over the years had become the prop and mainstay of the Mortimer household, having first entered it as Camilla's governess. When Camilla was promoted to a boarding school Tilly had stayed on as housekeeper to old Mr. Mortimer and latterly as Secretary-Companion to his widow. However, since Edna's correspondence was virtually restricted to turning down requests for money and her need for human companionship practically nonexistent, Tilly naturally had time to carry out a number of more menial tasks than the title implied.

"Tilly won't mind waiting," Camilla said airily, "she's quite used to that sort of thing."

"Except that she may think we've forgotten and driven home without her. Or is she quite used to that sort of thing too?"

"Stop bickering, children!" Vi said. "There's no need for it, no problem at all. Tell us which roundabout and we'll collect Tilly and take her home. It's perfectly simple."

Camilla supplied the details and two minutes later we were on our way, me in the back seat for the return journey.

The immediate destination was about ten minutes' drive from the course, during which Vi and Marge kept up a rattling non-stop dialogue. It is rarely easy to keep track of a conversation between close relatives when they really go at it, and was made harder still this time by their having their backs to me, so that I really had to strain to catch every word.

"Not a very happy pair of lovebirds this evening," Marge began by saying.

"No; pity if that's breaking down. Seemed such a good idea at first. Nice, dull, well connected local boy; reasonable sort of prospects; and high time he cut loose from his mother's apron strings, as we've all been saying these many years. Probably be the making of him. Even old Edna approved, so I can't see any reason for these clouds on the horizon, can you?"

"Unless it's because, despite having given them her blessing, Edna has not been handing out any lolly and has made it clear that she doesn't intend to."

"How do you know that?"

"Told me so herself. Said she believed in young people making their own way in the world. Learning the value of money before they got their hands on it, all that guff. As though anyone could find out the value of money until they've got some!"

"So that could be at the bottom of this rift, if rifts do have bottoms? Bernard marrying for money, or urged on to do so by his Mum, and then finding he wasn't going to get any?"

"No, to be fair, I don't think he's that low. Camilla's the one who's always had this obsession about money. It wouldn't surprise me if she'd worked out that the best way to persuade Edna to part with it was to make a respectable marriage with the boy next door and now it's she who's disappointed. I mean, even worse in a way to marry somebody for what you considered was your own money and then discover that he wasn't going to get it for you. I think this must be our roundabout coming up now, don't you, Tessa?" Marge added, turning round unexpectedly and causing me to rock back rather abruptly into a more conventional sitting position. "Didn't Camilla say the first one after the second set of traffic lights?"

"That's right. You're supposed to take the Reading turn-off and then stop twenty yards up the road at the bus shelter. Let's hope she's still there."

"Oh, she'll be there, never fear," Vi said. "On that you can rely."

She was right too. Tilly was not only at her post, but managed to give the impression of one who, having the choice, would have elected to while away a hot afternoon in a bus shelter on a noisy main road. Surrounded by bulging carrier bags, she sat with ankles crossed, deep in one-sided conversation with a bemused looking old man and stitching away at a square of pale blue material. When she joined me on the back seat I saw that it was a tray-cloth, which she was embroidering with scalloped edges, goodness knows why.

She briskly swept aside all the apologies and condolences showing far more concern for Camilla's plight than her own.

"Oh dear, oh dearie me!" she murmured when she had heard the full story. "How very unlucky! Now, wouldn't you think poor dear Camilla would know better by this time? I do hope they won't hang about too long."

"Why? What do you suppose can have happened?" I asked.

"Well dear, if the truth be known, I don't doubt that Mrs. Mortimer is half way home by now. Arrive before we do, I shouldn't wonder."

"How would she get there, though?"

"Oh, that wouldn't be much trouble. I expect she's run into one or two acquaintances during the afternoon and perhaps one of them was driving home in this direction."

"Do you mean it? You think she's got a lift with someone else? Then why not have found the others and told them so? I don't imagine they'd have minded."

"Very likely not, but that might have been a bit awkward. Poor Mrs. Mortimer!" Tilly added with a long sigh, which mystified me still further. Marge, however, appeared to be *au courant*, for she looked up and grinned into the rear mirror.

"But why . . . ?" I began, but just too late because simultaneously Tilly patted my arm affectionately, saying:

"So the Festival is on again, Tessa? Isn't that splendid news?"

"Isn't it just? How did you hear?"

"I met Helena while I was having my hair done. She'd popped in there to get them to display one of the posters, and she told me the glad tidings. So now you'll be a busy bee again? Camilla told me you had a leading part in your cousin's play?"

"Yes, I can't claim that he wrote it specially for me, but at least he knew better than to leave me out. Where should we be without a little nepotism to help us along life's hard road?"

"Will you be staying on with Toby?" Vi asked, also addressing the rear mirror.

"After we open. A lot depends on Robin's movements, but I'll probably commute from London during rehearsals."

"You can drop me off here, Vi," Tilly said, as we slowed down at the gates of Farndale House, which was the name of Edna's large Victorian residence. "No need to come up the drive. I've taken you too far out of your way already."

Vi and Marge both tried to talk her out of this attitude, arguing that she would have to carry her heavy parcels at least another hundred yards, but Tilly was adamant and eventually got her way.

"What did she mean by saying that it would be awkward for Edna to explain that she was getting a lift home with someone else?" I asked, as Vi turned the car in the direction of Roakes Common.

"Perhaps we shouldn't say, seeing that she obviously regretted having been so indiscreet."

"But we can't very well not tell her," Marge objected, to my great relief. "Or she'll invent some terribly sinister explanation of her own. At least, I know I should. You see, Tessa, Edna is not only one of Nature's foremost liars, but she always has to appear to be in the right. It wouldn't occur to her to walk up to someone and ask for a lift, on the grounds that Bernard's car was rather small and uncomfortable. That might show her up in a bad light. So it would all be wrapped up in some tale of having been cruelly let down, the most likely version in this case being that the young people had forgotten all about her and whisked off on their own. At which point, it would be an awkward business to find them and explain, would it not?"

"Yes, very, but I'm still baffled. Could she really be so selfish and unkind as to leave them dangling in the car park, not knowing what had become of her? It's incredible!"

"And it may not be true," Vi pointed out. "We are only telling you what had obviously occurred to Tilly. But she should know and the fact is that you can't expect rational behaviour from Edna. She's in a different category from the rest of us, and the most dangerous one of all."

"Which is that?"

"Well, lying comes naturally to her, for one thing, so even when there's nothing to gain by it she prevaricates instinctively; and as soon as it's uttered, to her it becomes the truth. She wouldn't feel any remorse for Bernard and Camilla because by the time her sad tale was out she'd believe every word of it."

"She has another trick, too," Marge said, sounding amused. "Even when she is telling the truth, she invariably lies about its source. I remember her giving me a recipe for a cold pudding, which could be knocked up in about ten minutes. Very good it was, too. I've used it in several crises. Edna told me she got it as a special favour from the chef at the Dorchester, but a few days later I was sitting under the hair dryer, reading one of those women's weeklies and there it was, tucked away among the readers' letters. It had won the two pound prize for Best Tip of the Week."

"It's rather pathetic, in a way," Vi remarked.

"Do you think so? I'd say she ought to be locked up."

Rather surprisingly, Marge countered this with a rare philosophical observation:

"And so she is, my child. Locked up inside her own fantasies, where everything in life is distorted. That's what is pathetic about it."

CHAPTER FOUR

•

1

Fantasy or not, Edna's own explanation for her temporary disappearance was far more sensational than those which others had invented on her behalf. As relayed by Marge on the telephone that evening, the story was as follows:

Immediately after the third race, which she had been watching from the stand with Camilla, Bernard having slumped off in a sulk to the bar, she had set off towards the pay-out windows to collect her winnings on Bitter Aloes. Camilla had accompanied her part of the way, but had then met some friends and, seeming disposed to stop and chat and to be quite oblivious of Edna's understandable impatience, she had proceeded on her own.

On reaching her destination, she had paused on the fringes, in order to size up the length of the various queues, meaning to attach herself to the shortest of them and, in so doing, had received one of the most disagreeable shocks of her whole life. At the head of one of the queues, and in the act of counting up her winnings, was a woman who, to her appalled amazement, she had instantly recognised as none other than herself. Too shocked to move or cry out, she had closed her eyes and clutched at one of the posts, in an effort to get a grip on things, and when she had forced herself to look up again she had found that the apparition, if such it was, had vanished and every-

18

thing, with the exception of her own heart rate, was back to normal.

"What made her think it was herself she saw?" I asked at this point.

"The whole works, apparently. You name it. Same coat and hat, same build and stance and, so far as she could judge in the time, same age as well. Now, why I've rung you up, Tessa, is this: Vi and I are completely flummoxed this time and we simply can't make up our minds whether to believe her or not. I mean, you can't exactly say the story rings true, but it's out of line with her usual fantasies and one can't immediately see any advantage in inventing it. Now, you had the winner of that race, didn't you? Did you happen to catch sight of this *doppelgänger*?"

"I'm afraid not, Marge, but that doesn't disprove her story. She was already there, pressed up against the window by the time I arrived, so the double, if she existed, would have gone by then. Edna obviously wasn't so knocked out that she forgot to collect her winnings."

"That doesn't prove anything either. It would take more than her own ghost to make her forget that. Did she seem frightened or upset in any way?"

I considered my answer carefully: "Well, you know, looking back on it, I honestly believe she did behave like someone who'd had some kind of shock. At the time, I put it down to her normal truculence, plus the fact that she was so unsuitably dressed for a warm afternoon, but it could well have been something more serious. All the same, I still don't see that it excuses her driving off and leaving Bernard and Camilla stranded."

"Well, according to Edna, it excuses her up to the hilt, because there seem to have been repercussions. She told Tilly that a little later on, she's not sure how much later, but possibly half an hour, she had some kind of black out. A heart attack is how she describes it, needless to say, but Tilly does think it's quite on the cards that she'd had a very mild stroke. Luckily, she was sitting down, so there was no fall or anything, but Edna says that when she came to there was no one in sight and she didn't know where she was, or what had happened to her; but she felt too weak to move and absolutely positive she was dying. And it is true that she was in a pretty groggy state when they found her."

"Who did find her, by the way?"

"People called Powell. I don't suppose you know them? He's a brigadier, got a stiff leg and they live not far from Datchet, so it meant going miles out of their way to bring her home, but apparently they didn't hesitate. So it can't have been all invention on her part and, frankly, I don't think she has the imagination to dream up anything so dramatic."

"Has she seen her doctor?"

"No, Tilly sent for him, but it's his weekend off. His partner would have come, but she's a woman and Edna wasn't having any of that. I suppose her own doctor will look in on Monday, but she'll probably be over it by then. It's disappointing that you can't shed any light."

"Awfully sorry, Marge, but if I do get a total recall I'll ring you back."

"Yes, do; and in the meantime there's an outsider in the Derby called Spittin Image. Better have a go, wouldn't you say?"

"Why not? It was really all due to Edna that I backed Bitter Aloes, so perhaps she'll pull it off again."

2

I had scarcely put the receiver down when the telephone rang again and this time it was Camilla on the line. She was calling principally to enlist my help in finding her a job connected in some way with the Storhampton Festival, but before we got down to that I had to hear the tale of Edna's misadventure all over again, as I did not consider it diplomatic to disclose that Marge had got in first.

Camilla's version differed hardly at all from the first one, but provided a small bonus in that it had a sequel. It appeared that the doctor's lady partner having rung him up and explained matters, he had dropped his golf clubs where he stood and hurried round to visit the patient in person. Edna had been neither surprised nor particularly gratified by this gesture, for it was precisely what she had expected and, had it been otherwise, would doubtless have signed on with a rival practitioner, which, according to Camilla, was something she did rather frequently.

"And what was his diagnosis?" I asked.

"Well, he didn't seem to think there was any special cause for alarm, only her blood pressure's much too high and she's badly overweight and so on. All the usual things that we know already, in fact, but he did warn me that it makes her vulnerable to this sort of attack and she might get another, and much worse one, any time at all. Anyway, he's given me a prescription which I can collect from the surgery, and he's also put her on a very strict diet and told me to see that she gets plenty of rest. So it looks as though I'll be stuck down here for the time being and I'll go raving mad if I don't have something to do."

It was at this point that she introduced her bid for my help in finding her some voluntary work with the Festival, but before dealing with it, I said:

"But why you, Camilla? Isn't it the moment for that old sister to come and lend a hand?"

"Alice? Oh, sure! She'd grab at the chance to dig herself in here, but it would be fatal. Sister or not, Edna can't stand having her to stay for even one night. She's too mean, for one thing, and Alice eats like a horse. She'd be worse than useless in a situation like this."

"Then can't Tilly manage on her own?"

"No, she can't. It's all very well for you to say that, but poor Tilly is imposed on quite enough already. She's taken on most of the cooking and housework, as it is, and now Edna's talking about cutting the gardener down to two mornings a week. This would be an excuse to load even more on to Tilly. She'd have her waiting on her hand and foot in no time at all."

These were admirable sentiments, but I was not moved to tears by them. For one thing, it was hard to see how she could materially ease the burden on Tilly if she was going to be slogging away at the Festival headquarters most of the day. On the other hand, it was not for me to turn down such an offer when the organisers were screaming for helpers, so I said that I envisaged no difficulty in fixing her up in some capacity or other, providing she wasn't too choosy about it, and she said she supposed not and rang off without bothering to thank me.

"Tell me something, Toby," I said at dinner that evening. "If you were going about your innocent business and suddenly saw someone whom you recognised as yourself, would you have a heart attack?"

"Yes, instantly."

"Indeed? You sound very positive, but how can you tell? I mean, it's not a thing that has ever happened to you, presumably?"

"There are some things one doesn't need to experience in order to gauge one's reactions and I can assure you, with no hesitation at all that if I were to look up now and see myself walking into the room you would have to telephone for the ambulance."

"Oh yes, I quite agree, but I wasn't thinking of a head-on confrontation. In the case which prompted this enquiry the victim didn't come face to face with herself, she only saw her back and it wasn't all that close."

"Nevertheless, she was convinced it was her own back?"

"That's right."

"And what happened?"

"Nothing. Herself got away."

"Do you know, I think that might make it even more alarming," Toby said seriously. "On the whole, it might be better to thrash the matter out on the spot and decide once and for all which was the alter and which the ego. One could never tell what he might get up to, if one were to lose track of him."

"True! I hadn't thought of that."

"Better not dwell on it. The whole concept is so macabre that I think we should change the subject. Otherwise, I may easily bring on a heart attack just by thinking about it."

CHAPTER FIVE

•

The reality of a Storhampton Festival of Music and the Arts had come about largely through the inspiration and tenacity of a couple named Goodchild, who, as so often in matters of community endeavour, were comparative new-comers to the neighbourhood.

Peter Goodchild was senior music master at a nearby public school and his wife, Tara, a towering and bossy intellectual, who spent a lot of time translating obscure Bengali poets into every language under the sun. They had two emaciated looking daughters, both with impecca-ble manners, who romped through every exam they sat for, scooping up scholarships like pebbles off the beach.

The enterprise had been conceived by the Goodchilds some three years before its inception, in those days as a relatively modest, strictly amateur venture, to coincide with the Summer Regatta, but had gained momentum from two unexpected windfalls. The first concerned an abandoned Victorian Methodist Chapel, close to the cen-tre of the town and even closer to the river, which came on the market at a more or less giveaway price and which Peter Goodchild reckoned could be transformed, with a little unpaid weekend help from his pupils, into a very presentable concert hall.

The second factor exerted its influence more gradually, for, as their acquaintance widened, they found themselves on visiting terms with no fewer than three resident profes-

sional authors, two poets, any number of actors and amateur painters and one real live composer. Fired by this,
the flame of a full scale Festival of the Arts began to burn
brightly in the Goodchild hearts and, being tireless and
enthusiastic to a degree unparalleled in those parts, eventually overcame every obstacle which faintheartedness and
lethargy could place in their way. Local traders and cater-
ers were dragooned or flattered into putting up contributions, local talent found itself offering its services free and,
greatest achievement of all, the Town Hall was somehow
persuaded to match the total raised with an equivalent
sum from municipal funds.

In the ensuing, highly charged months of meetings,
decisions, counter decisions, triumphs, disasters and res-
ignations, the final programme eventually emerged, trimmed
and dented here and there, but in essence very much as
the instigators had conceived it. It was to run for three
weeks from mid-July, opening with an evening concert by
the County Youth Orchestra, Peter Goodchild conducting,
and winding up with a midnight fireworks display on the
river. The filling between these two slices of the sandwich
was to include an art exhibition, poetry readings, a ball at
the Town Hall and three specially commissioned plays,
running in repertory at the converted Methodist Chapel.

Sadly, however, extraneous events had moved faster
than the Festival Committee and, by the time their plans
were finally hatched, inflation had ensured that there would
not be half enough money to carry them out. Bloody but
unbowed, the Goodchilds had fought on regardless and an
appeal fund, aimed at the general public, had been set up.
This had raised a few more thousands, but it was still not
enough and, six weeks before the scheduled opening, it
had been announced that the Festival would be postponed
until the following year, by which time it would have been
pruned to more modest proportions and would be spread
over a single week. It was at this point that the benefactor
from London had stepped in so dramatically and saved the
day.

My principal informant in these matters had been Helena Plowman, the Hon. Treasurer and wife of Storhamp-

ton's leading solicitor, and it was therefore to her that I now applied on Camilla's behalf.

Instead of falling over herself with gratitude and delight, as I had expected, she sent me spinning back on my heels by demanding to know why Camilla had not approached her direct, adding in a highly aggrieved tone:

"Since she is officially engaged to my son, you'd think that would be the normal way to go about it."

"Well, honestly, Helena, now you mention it, I simply can't imagine why she didn't. I knew Bernard was your son, of course, but somehow the two things hadn't connected. It comes of keeping one's professional life in a separate compartment, I suppose. Perhaps she was under the impression that in view of the relationship it wouldn't be ethical to ask you."

"But that's absurd."

"Yes, it is; so I can only think that she was really angling for a job in the theatre and hadn't the nerve to come straight out with it."

"Would there be anything for her there?"

"Absolutely not. She's had no experience. She'd be worse than useless."

"In that case, I suppose I'll have to see what I can find for her. I happen to know that Debbie Fox, who's in charge of the press and publicity, is at her wits' end for volunteers. The trouble there is that it involves a good deal of leg work, and I don't see that going down very well, do you?"

"Quite honestly, no; but perhaps she could get her hands on a car? What sort of job would it be?"

"I gather from Debbie the most urgent thing is to make a round of all the hotels and restaurants and persuade them to buy advertising space in the programmes and souvenir books."

"I thought the programmes had already been made up?"

"So they had, but luckily they'd only reached the proof stage when the thing collapsed on us, so there's still time to rake in a few more, if you really think Camilla's serious about wanting to help."

I declared emphatically that such was my belief and, having tendered my profuse thanks, rang up Camilla to pass on the good news, which got the most snooty reception imaginable. I eventually managed to calm her down by stressing the importance of the job, which Debbie Fox, whoever she might be, would entrust to no other, but it was uphill work and the most irritating part of all was that I could not see what the hell I had to apologise for.

It was not an unfamiliar position to be in, but one of the worst examples of its kind and I made a solemn vow with myself never to lift a finger again on behalf of any of the Mortimer clan, come what might. What did come, however, and in a matter of weeks, was a complete reversal of this sensible resolution.

CHAPTER SIX

•

Toby's play, specially commissioned by the Festival for a
fee of nothing, had been carefully constructed to suit the
limitations of a converted Methodist Chapel, as well as to
strike a topical note.

It was a comedy with five characters, four of whom were
leading lights of an amateur dramatic society, rehearsing a
production which was to be part of a local Festival of the
Arts, and the fifth being a professional actor imported for
the occasion from London.

If this sounds confusing, I have drawn the picture accu-
rately and it also imposed rather a heavy strain on most of
the cast. The difference between a professional and an
amateur at work may be subtle, but it is instantly recognisable to most audiences and it is not too paradoxical to
suggest that a trained actor has as much difficulty in portraying a gifted amateur as the least gifted amateur would
have in portraying Juliet on her balcony.

Since much of the comedy depended for its effect on
these very nuances, it was not an undertaking to be treated
lightly and the tough going at rehearsals, combined with
the fifty mile drive to and from London every day, temporarily cut me off from everything and everyone not connected with either Beacon Square, S.W.1., where Robin
and I lived, or the interior of the Chapel.

During this period the weird goings-on at Farndale
House lost most of their former impact and I rarely gave

them a thought; but after two weeks of this grind there came an unexpected respite. Robin found that he had been selected to represent his division at a Police Conference in the north of England, which required him to be away for ten days. As a result of this, I moved in with Toby, which at least cut down the commuting distance to ten miles a day and, by a coincidence, this occurred just after a second, rather more disquieting incident concerning Edna and her double, although as before, opinions varied as to its authenticity, since there had been no other witness.

It was Camilla's version that I heard first. Evidently she had done rather better as an advertising saleswoman than either Helena or I had predicted and had recently been promoted to Assistant Press Officer. Her new job entailed working the editors of all the local papers into a white heat of excitement by bombarding them with photographs and thumbnail sketches of Festival "personalities" and she had come to the theatre to conduct some interviews with the cast.

For obvious reasons, I was the guinea-pig in this enterprise and when I had filled her in with some missing items in the curriculum vitae, which did not appear to impress her very much, we repaired to the coffee shop on the corner, so that I could prime her on the kind of questions she should ask in forthcoming interviews.

"Thanks, Tessa, that's all quite useful," she said when we had concluded this business, adding with a mournful, martyred sigh, "I just hope I'll be able to carry on doing it, that's all."

"Oh, I shouldn't worry. It's not all that difficult to get people to talk about themselves, especially actors. All you've got to do is hit on a theme, create an image out of it and make sure everything you report them as saying helps to build it up. It doesn't matter in the least how true it is, so long as they're flattered by it and go along with you."

"Yes, yes, I'm sure you're right," she said impatiently, "and it sounds absolutely dead simple, but the trouble is that I may have to pack it in before I've even got going."

Having warmed to her, as one does to people who come begging for advice and then actually appear to listen to it, I now found all the old hostility flowing back, with compound interest.

"Well, I like that, Camilla! What the hell have I been wasting my time for, if you intend to throw the job up?"

"I don't want to throw the job up, of course not, but I may have no choice. There are so many outside pressures."

"What outside pressures?"

"Well, Bernard's not desperately pleased about my using his car so much, for one; but Edna is the main problem. She's had another of these hallucinations, or whatever they are, and it's fairly knocked her sideways this time."

"When was this?"

"Yesterday morning."

"And she saw her own double again?"

"So she claims. No one can make much sense of it, but something has certainly upset her pretty badly. Dr. Martin is quite worried this time. He hinted that she couldn't possibly be faking her symptoms, so if she gets another of these turns I may be forced to resign, which is pretty bloody disheartening."

Camilla appeared to have forgotten that she had only taken the job in the first place as an adjunct to being on hand to help look after Edna and to have become more concerned with the means than the end, but I did not remind her of this, not wishing to antagonise her until I had elicited a few details.

"But do tell me what happened? Where did she see the creature this time?"

"In the garden, of all places."

"What was she doing in the garden?"

"Wandering about as though she owned the place, according to Edna. That's probably what brought on the seizure. I expect she was scared out of her mind that this woman was pinching the lettuces or something. No, I oughtn't to be so unkind! It must have been a pretty ghastly experience, whether she imagined it or not."

"So no one else saw anything?"

"No, I was at the office and Tilly had nipped down to

the village. She was gone about twenty minutes and when she got back and went into the garden to see if Edna needed anything she found her practically in a state of collapse; panting and groaning and carrying on like a mad thing."

"What was the woman wearing? Fur coat and green velvet turban?"

"No, quite ordinarily dressed, I gather, in a skirt and cardigan and sort of blue linen sun hat."

"Closely resembling a skirt and cardigan of Edna's, no doubt?"

"Not just resembling, she swears they were her own."

"So she was close enough to tell that? Did she see her face this time?"

"Only in a blurred kind of way. The hat hid most of it, whereas Edna had the sun full in her eyes. Also she was probably going rapidly into a state of shock. She was practically unconscious when Tilly found her."

"One other thing, though, Camilla: did anyone think of checking her wardrobe to see if those particular clothes were missing?"

"Not that I know of. You have to remember that it was quite a while before she was able to tell anyone what had happened. Tilly managed to bring her round a bit with what she called routine first aid. She's a marvel, old Tilly, the way she rallies so calmly in every emergency. Then she telephoned Dr. Martin, who said he'd be round as quick as he could, but in the meantime Edna ought to be moved into the house, or at any rate a shadier part of the garden. It was quite a problem, that, because of course Tilly couldn't possibly manage it on her own. Edna weighs a ton, as you can imagine. She tried to get hold of me, but unfortunately I was out on a job. Then she rang Bernard's office to see if he could oblige, but that was no go either because he had to spend yesterday morning at the Reading Assizes. Anyway, the doctor had turned up by then and between them they managed to haul Edna upstairs, and he gave her an injection. She was sleeping when I came back at lunchtime, so there was no point in my hanging around and, as I'd made all these appointments for today,

Tilly absolutely insisted on my sticking to them. So what I do now is ring her up every couple of hours, to check that everything's okay, but, honestly, I can't see how we can go on like this indefinitely, never knowing when or where this ghost is going to bob up next, not even knowing for sure whether Edna imagined it."

"Still, I can't see what good you'll do by stopping at home; not unless you're prepared to watch her every minute of the day."

"Why not?"

"Because, obviously, if she had dreamt or invented it, she's not going to be seeing any phantoms when there's a witness around. On the other hand, if it's true and there really is a living human being who is carrying out this persecution campaign, she will be equally careful not to manifest herself when there's someone else there, specially someone young and active like yourself. The success of the operation would depend entirely on keeping her identity secret; but nobody can be guarded for twenty-four hours a day and, sooner or later Edna will have to be left on her own. Then, if she has another of these visitations, you'll be no better off than you were before."

"Okay, since you're so jolly clever," Camilla said, reverting to the snarling exchanges of our childhood, "perhaps you'd care to make a suggestion of your own, instead of always criticising other people's."

"As it happens, I would. If I were you, Camilla, I'd begin at the other end. Forget about Edna, for the time being and concentrate on keeping a close watch on her wardrobe."

CHAPTER SEVEN

•

After all, Camilla was not obliged to sacrifice her job,
because a few days after the foregoing conversation Fer-
nando Benjamin Mortimer, otherwise known as Ferdy,
arrived at Farndale House. He was Camilla's uncle, although only seven or eight years her senior, being the son
and only child of her grandfather's short-lived second marriage. He was an amiable, moon-faced young man, viewed
with disfavour on account of his feckless ways by nearly
everyone except Tilly, whose indulgence knew no limits,
and by Vi and Marge, who were prepared to grant a
reasonable amount of it to anyone who shared their pas-
sion for racing.

I had been told that he earned a living of sorts, drifting
from one undemanding job to another and regularly de-
positing the weekly pay packet at the nearest betting shop
every Saturday morning, but, apart from this absorbing
interest, was without ties of any kind and therefore usually
able to step into whatever breach required him, provided
it required no special skill or energy.

The ostensible breach this time was the Farndale garden, which, in this mild early summer season, was rapidly
getting choked with weeds and long grass and needing far
more attention than could be bestowed upon it by a gardener on two mornings a week, even when supplemented
by the odd hours which Tilly was able to contribute.

Ferdy had declared himself able and willing to lend a

hand and Edna had raised no objection, since however much she might openly despise him, he was one of the few people who neither argued with her, nor cast doubts on her tall stories. More important still, he was prepared to give up three or four weeks to weeding, mowing and clipping, simply in return for his board and lodging, and this was a bargain she could not resist.

Unknown to her, of course, his real function was to provide an extra pair of eyes to watch over her and in an area, moreover, where she was most vulnerable and could most easily escape Tilly's vigilance.

Camilla had claimed full credit for this scheme, but I suspected that it had originated with Tilly, who was past master at planting ideas in other people's heads and then falling over herself with admiration when they brought them out as their own, for the truth was that a certain coolness had always existed between Ferdy and Camilla. I had attributed this mainly to there being something naturally uncongenial, even ridiculous, in an uncle/niece relationship when the age difference is so negligible, but there was more to it than this, as I was shortly to learn from Vi and Marge.

They had invited me to another meeting and, on learning to their horrified amazement that neither Saturdays, holidays nor even racing days were exempt from the grind of rehearsals, had suggested that I should dine with them instead, so that at least I could obtain a first hand account of the day's sport. Toby, having also been invited, had also accepted. This was a rare concession for him, for it was his invariable rule not to dine out if he could possibly avoid it, but he made an exception of Vi and Marge. For one thing, they were superlative cooks and also possessed a first class cellar, lovingly put together by Marge's bombastic husband and now coming into its own; but the most persuasive point of all in their favour was his well founded belief that neither of them had the least desire to marry him.

All this just compensated for the undeniable fact that they could be rather boring about the horses they had backed, failed to back or been tempted to back, and the sums won and lost if only they had followed their hunches, or only not done so, but for once even this price was waived because another topic took precedence. Edna had also been at the meeting, accompanied by Ferdy, and there had been a fresh episode in her supernatural life, which, from one point of view, appeared as a breakthrough and, from another, as merely adding to the confusion. In short, the double had manifested herself again, although without the devastating effect of the two previous occasions. Edna was now no longer haunted by the fear that she was, as she put it, "seeing things" for the simple reason that Ferdy had been seeing them too. The only drawback was that they had seen them on separate occasions and they were not identically the same things. However, as Vi reminded us, due allowance had to be made for the fallibility of all witnesses, and never more so than in the case of Edna and her stepson.

Ferdy's experience was as follows:

Around the middle of the afternoon he had escorted Edna to the outdoor bar, which was situated midway between the paddock and the Tote and, having installed her at a table for two, went up to the counter to order their drinks. There was a great mob of thirst maddened racegoers already congregated there, and a staff of only two to deal with them and, not being one of Nature's pushers, it had taken him a full five minutes to reach the front ranks. Having achieved this much, he had looked sideways along the counter, hoping to attract the barmaid's attention, when, to his mild annoyance, he had seen his stepmother right at the far end and already being served.

The reaction was no stronger than this because being kept waiting was not an affliction which she suffered gracefully and such behaviour was fairly typical, except that it was somewhat unprecedented for her to pay for her own drinks when not absolutely obliged to. However, since, in the perverse way of bar attendants, this one had now noticed him and was asking for his order, he did not like to tell her that he was only looking, and went ahead with Edna's instructions.

When he carried the glasses over to the table Edna was

sitting exactly where he had left her, tapping her feet and complaining bitterly about his sloth and inefficiency. Her bag, race card and newspaper were on the table, which was otherwise bare.

Slightly perturbed by this direct contradiction to the evidence of his own eyes, Ferdy had borne her reproaches in silence, but a little later in the afternoon some dark clouds had appeared overhead and she had despatched him to fetch her umbrella from the car. He was rather hazy about its position in the car park, which at this time was jammed to capacity and admitted having been away a good ten minutes, which was probably an understatement. He had left Edna sitting at the same table as they had used before and when he returned at last she was in very poor shape indeed, gasping for breath and with tears running down her face, while two bewildered, embarrassed Samaritans stood about making tentative efforts to discover what was the matter. With deep relief, they handed the responsibility over to Ferdy, who had already guessed what the matter was and lost no time in telling her of his own experience.

Needless to say, Edna was wonderfully cheered up by this and was able calmly to relate how, during his absence, as she scanned the crowd for his return, she had seen a woman walking away from the paddock, who was of course herself. Her relief at finding she was neither mad, nor suffering from hallucinations, was so overpowering that she gladly accepted Ferdy's explanation of the phenomenon, namely, that the woman was no figment of anyone's imagination, nor spectre either, but quite simply Edna's sister, Alice, wearing some of Edna's cast off clothing. The only thing that puzzled him was that no one had thought of this before.

As a matter of fact, several people had thought of it before, but had instantly dismissed the thought. Apart from the pointlessness of such childish goings-on, there was only a superficial resemblance between them, Alice being notably thinner and sharper featured. As for the clothes she had been described as wearing on each of her appearances on the race course, these provided the clearest evidence of all in her favour. While it was entirely credible that Edna would have flogged a shabby skirt and linen sun hat to her sister, sooner than give them away to a jumble sale, it was quite inconceivable that she would have done the same with a mink coat. However worn and outdated, the price Edna would have put on it would have been far beyond Alice's means.

Nevertheless, Ferdy's cheerful insistence that it must have been Alice he saw gave me a new idea, or rather strengthened one which had been floating around ever since my talk with Camilla and during our dinner table discussion I said to Vi:

"Tell me some more about Alice. Where does she live?"

"Not far away. Egham, I think, or it might be Datchet; somewhere like that."

"Ever been married?"

"No, old maid, like me. She used to be Matron of a hospital somewhere in those parts. Retired about a year ago."

"So not too well off?"

"I don't see how anyone could be too well off," Toby objected.

"And Alice certainly doesn't qualify," Vi said. "She'd have a pension, of course, and she takes a few private patients for physio-therapy, what they used to call massage in my day. Probably stashed a bit away too, if it runs in the family; but still a pauper by Edna's standards. Why do you want to know?"

"Perhaps Tessa is wondering, as I am," Toby suggested, "why a woman of straitened means, probably with as little interest in racing as I have, should be prancing around in the Members' Enclosure."

"So am I," Marge admitted. "Puzzled to death by it. I've never seen her there once and I feel sure Ferdy's got it all wrong, as usual."

"She needn't necessarily have been in the expensive part, though," I pointed out. "If you have a mind to, you can get to the paddock and that cafeteria from anywhere on the course, even for free, if you can put up with the long walk."

"That's true," Vi admitted. "And if she had, it would account for the fact that neither Edna nor Ferdy saw her more than once. Otherwise, they'd surely have caught sight of her at other times and so should we. Tessa's right and she has cleared up one small mystery."

"She may have done so for you," Toby remarked. "Personally, I am still 'Yours sincerely, Baffled'. Are we to understand that she is behaving in this eccentric fashion for the express purpose of frightening her sister into a fatal heart attack? Or is she merely the innocent racegoer who happens to share her sister's taste in clothes? In which case, what was she doing flitting about in the sister's garden in that furtive fashion? And, whatever answer you give me, it still won't explain how she got her hands on a mink coat."

"Perhaps your two questions cancel each other out?" I suggested.

"They may well do. I am afraid I have rather lost track. What does their cancellation leave us with?"

"Well, say she'd borrowed one of the minks to go racing in, without Edna's permission? Flitting about in the garden could just have been her way of seeing if the coast was clear to put it back. Naturally, when she saw Edna sitting there, she flitted away again with all speed, doing the switch on a later occasion."

There was qualified approval for this theory, in so far as everyone else was stumped for a more plausible one and, considering it best to rest on these very flimsy laurels, I was then prompted to ask Vi what had started the feud between Camilla and her Uncle Ferdy and why they were now outwardly reconciled.

"Well, it was always on her side, you know. Ferdy is much too lazy to quarrel with anyone, but Camilla was always a jealous little monkey, even as a child, and she resented parting with half her inheritance."

"From her grandfather?"

"Yes. When her parents died in the air crash he became her legal guardian and it was understood that everything would go to her on his death. His second wife had already left him, by that time. He'd settled a fairly good whack on her, in trust for the boy, so Ferdy would have been well provided for. Unfortunately for Camilla. . . ."

"He decided to get his hands on a bit more?"

"Not on your life. He hasn't got an ounce of guile in him, silly old Ferdy! But when he was fourteen or so his mother married again and went back to Spain, where she'd come from in the first place. Naturally, Ferdy wasn't keen to switch to a Spanish school, he had enough trouble keeping up with the lessons in English. So, anyway, he was allowed to stay on where he was and, after one rather disastrous holiday in Madrid, he took to spending most of them with his father."

"Thus putting Camilla's nose out of joint?"

"And she's never really succeeded in getting it straightened out again," Marge observed.

"It wasn't simply that she was no longer Grandpa's and Tilly's one and only pet lamb," Vi explained. "There was worse to come because Ferdy's mother started a new family, rather late in life, and more or less lost interest in her first born; or perhaps an adolescent boy was rather an embarrassment to her at that point. Anyway, she bowed out of the custody and Ferdy was legally returned to his father. You can guess what followed?"

"A new division of his property, I suppose?"

"Just so. Share and share alike and fair do's all round. Not that it matters any more. As we all know, a year or two later he married Edna, who got the lot; and I daresay neither of the former heirs will ever see a penny of it. She's quite capable of leaving it all to a cat's home."

"A mink farm might be more appropriate," Toby suggested.

Apparently, it did not occur to anyone except myself that she might equally well have left it all to her sister, Alice.

CHAPTER EIGHT

•

The curtain went up on our opening performance at seven o'clock, or as near as makes no difference, on the second evening of the Festival, which was also the occasion of the Mayor's Ball, but Toby steered clear of both functions. He never attends his own first nights, airily proclaiming himself to be indifferent to success and failure alike, but in reality, I suspect, rating one of those twin imposters too high above the other for his own comfort.

However, there was quite a scattering of old friends in front, including a small party from Farndale, and Bernard and Camilla came round to see me in my cubicle, in the converted vestry, after the show. Camilla was kind enough to tell me that she had enjoyed parts of it, but that, as far as she could tell, Edna hadn't laughed once.

"Oh, Edna's with you, is she? Are you taking her to the ball?"

"No, we're not. She was too mean to pay for her own ticket and, as no one seemed particularly keen to invite her, she said it would be too much excitement for one evening, so she's gone home."

"Rather rough on Ferdy?"

"Not at all. He's got off very lightly, as usual. Probably even now twirling round the floor in the arms of Tara Goodchild."

"You don't tell me you've gone and let Edna off the leash? What if she had another turn?"

"Oh, of course, you don't know, do you?" Camilla said with great disdain. "I always forget that you lot can't see the audience just as clearly as we can see you."

This was a non-sequitur, if ever I heard one, but Bernard elucidated:

"It was rather a joke, really. Old Tilly's idea, you may be sure. Ferdy was to have come with us, but then she had this inspiration about laying the ghost, as she puts it."

"Edna's ghost?"

"Right. And she made Ferdy give up his seat to sister Alice."

"That was risky, wasn't it?"

"She thought that bringing them together would help to create a normal atmosphere," Camilla said primly, "and rid Edna of this idiotic idea that Alice is going around impersonating her. That's where Tilly is so marvellous. She really worries about Edna you know and, in spite of everything, I believe she's genuinely fond of her."

"And did the plan work?"

"I couldn't tell you, really," she replied, losing interest, "they seemed to be arguing most of the time. Still, you could say that was normal enough, so I expect Tilly was on the right lines. Anyway, the good news, from our point of view, is that Alice has now taken Edna home and, as she's a trained nurse, she ought to be able to handle Sis, if she starts falling apart again. Do you want a lift to the Town Hall?"

"No thanks. A bunch of us from here are going together. Might see you when we get there, though."

"I couldn't say about that, actually, Tessa. I've had a pretty heavy week and I've got to be up early in the morning," Camilla said, yawning at the prospect. "Bernard, too. All right for some! I suppose you can loll in bed till lunchtime, if you want to?"

"Teatime, if I want to. No performance to-morrow. The other lot get their turn."

"God, some people have it dead easy! Well, see you some time, I expect. Bernard's mother insists on our putting in an appearance at this ghastly do, but I certainly don't intend to stay for more than an hour."

* * *

Perhaps she was better than her word too, for I did not catch a glimpse of either of them, although arriving well within her deadline. If so, she probably earned another black mark from Helena, who was still there, with her husband and the rest of their party, when I packed it in just before midnight.

Nor was I permitted to stay in bed until teatime, or anywhere near it. Camilla made sure of that by telephoning before she left for work, to enlist my help. Edna had had another stroke and this time it was serious. She had lost her powers of speech and the whole of her left side was paralysed. Dr. Martin had promised to lay on a nurse as soon as he could, but in the meantime the patient was not to be left alone for a single minute. Camilla wanted me to go and sit with her for a couple of hours in the afternoon, to give Tilly a break.

When I asked her what had caused the stroke and when it had struck, so to speak, she grandly informed me that she was already due at her office and it was therefore not convenient to go into details, but that I should find out in due course.

So I rang up Tilly and told her to expect me at two o'clock.

CHAPTER NINE

•

1

The patient was asleep when I arrived. Tilly had left the front door on the latch and I had played too many games of hide and seek in that house not to be fully acquainted with the whereabouts of the principal bedroom. It was the one which had been out of bounds to us and was occupied in those days by Camilla's grandfather.

That door was open too and the only light inside came from the landing, the curtains of both windows being tightly drawn. Tilly was seated by the larger one, mending a sheet, a task which long practice had evidently enabled her to perform in near darkness. When she saw me she first put a finger to her lips in a warning gesture and then beckoned me to a second chair, which had been pulled up beside hers.

I had not dared so much as to glance in Edna's direction, but Tilly told me that she had been sleeping peacefully for about half an hour, no longer in the heavy coma in which they had first found her. There had also been one or two lucid moments and, generally, a slight improvement in her condition.

"Give me my instructions," I whispered.

"You can speak out loud, so long as you keep your voice down," Tilly answered in what I instantly recognised from a long while back as her governessy voice. "It's only the light which seems to bother her, it almost seems to drive her mad, but ordinary sounds make no impression. It would probably be safe for us to talk normally, except that she might wake up and hear what we were saying. One can't tell how much her hearing has been affected."

I was heartened by these words, as well as by the fact that Tilly had not put down her sewing, for they indicated that her departure was not imminent. Having a somewhat primitive fear of invalids, I had dreaded being left alone with this one, certain that she would inevitably make some demand on me which would show up my ineptitude. However, for form's sake I spoke my piece:

"Listen, Tilly, now that I'm here, why not let me hold the fort while you lie down for a bit? You must be worn out?"

"No, I'm not," she replied coolly. "Not in the least. It's really quite restful sitting here. In some ways, I'll be sorry when the nurse comes. Then I'll be back to the cooking and cleaning again, and waiting on her into the bargain, I shouldn't wonder."

Perversely, I had now begun to feel rather superfluous and, thoughtful as ever, she must have sensed this, for she patted my knee and said kindly:

"It was so good of you to come, Tessa, dear, and I do appreciate it. The only disagreeable thing about being chained to this room is the lack of company. I'd much sooner stay and have a little chat with you."

"You really do bear the brunt, don't you, Tilly?"

"Well, that's as it should be, my child. It's what I'm here for. Camilla would have stayed at home, if I'd asked her to, I haven't the least doubt of that, but this work she's doing for you all has come to mean so much to her and I don't believe in young people being sacrificed to the elderly. I saw too much of that in my own youth. Besides, she wouldn't really be much of a hand at this job, do you think? She does her best, poor girl, but she's too restless and excitable to be much use in a sick room. Not like you, but then you two always were chalk and cheese, weren't you?"

"I suppose so, although I doubt if I'm cut out to be a sick-room attendant either."

"Well, you've no need to worry on that account. I

shouldn't dream of leaving you here on your own, unless Mrs. Mortimer were well and truly asleep and then, if she should wake up or make any movement at all, you'd only have to call me and I'd be back in two shakes."

"When did this attack come on?"

Tilly sighed, then tilted her head to catch a sliver of light between the curtains, as she re-threaded her needle:

"That's just what we don't know, you see, that's the dreadful part of it. It could have been any time between about midnight, when Camilla came home, and seven o'clock this morning, when I found her lying there. Goodness, what a shock that was!"

"Lying where?"

"In the doorway, between her bathroom and the landing. Didn't Camilla tell you? What a strange girl she is sometimes! It was what upset me most of all, thinking of her lying there, all alone in the dark, conscious perhaps, but unable to call or move, while we all slept soundly in our beds. I've always felt sorry for old folks who have to live on their own, but it only shows that you can be in just as much trouble in a house full of people."

"What was she wearing when you found her?"

"Just her nightgown. She hadn't even stopped to put her slippers on. I suppose she was in a tearing hurry to get to the bathroom, poor dear. I was always on at old Mr. Mortimer to put in a bathroom adjoining this bedroom. It could easily have been converted from that little dressing room next door, which is no use for anything except my old sewing machine. Still, I daresay it wouldn't have made much difference."

"In other words, she'd been to bed and got up again?"

"Yes, we do know that much because otherwise Camilla would have found her, you see. She didn't get home until about an hour after her grandmother had gone upstairs, but it still leaves a fearfully long gap. It's a mystery to me why she didn't catch pneumonia, but luckily Dr. Martin thinks we're safely out of that wood!"

"Were you still awake when Alice brought her home?"

"Just about, but it was touch and go, I don't mind telling you. I'd promised to stay up until she came in, but

I had no end of a job to keep from dropping off. Being on the go all day and then just sitting down with nothing special to do, the hours seemed to drag. Luckily, the Plowmans looked in on their way to the Town Hall, which livened things up a bit. Bernard's parents, you know them?"

"Yes. That is, I know Helena. What did they come for?"

"Well, they knew they'd catch me on my own and Helena wanted to borrow my embroidery book. At least, that was the excuse, but I think the truth was that she'd got round Robert to take a look at our old vacuum cleaner."

"Why on earth should he want to do that?"

"He didn't want to, my dear, far from it; specially when he was all dressed up in his dinner jacket, poor man. But Helena's such a dear and she knew what a worry it was for me."

"Why? Has it gone wrong?"

"The motor keeps cutting out, tiresome old thing, it's been driving me wild. I unpicked the plug, but there was nothing wrong there. Then dear old Ferdy had a go at it, but he's not very mechanically minded and it played up worse than ever after that."

"But I don't understand, Tilly. Why on earth didn't you ring up the dealers or send for an electrician?"

"Ah well, you see, dear, it's not as simple as that, not in this household, at any rate. Mrs. Mortimer gets quite upset at having to pay for repairs of that sort and that wasn't good for her at all, in the state she was in, even before this last go. She said that, what with the V.A.T. and the man's time and all the rest of it, it would work out almost as expensive as buying a new machine, and I daresay it would."

"Then why not buy a new machine?"

Tilly sighed: "Yes, you'd think that might be the best solution, but the trouble is that Mrs. Mortimer has never had to do any housework herself, at any rate not for a good many years, and she can't understand how much time it takes up. When Ferdy tried to get round her to buy a new one she said it was quite unnecessary because the work could be done just as well, or better, with some elbow

grease and a good stiff brush. Ah well, I daresay it will
have to come to that before much longer. Robert did his
best, but he said that what it really needs is a new motor."

"What a shame! But, to get back to Mrs. Mortimer, was
she all right when she came home from the theatre?"

"Right as rain. I'd just gone upstairs to slip on a dressing
gown, but I heard the door, so I went down again at
once."

"Did Alice come in with her?"

"Oh no, dear. One evening together would have been
quite long enough for those two. Neither of them would
have been anxious to prolong it. At least, if Alice did just
see her into the house, as she'd promised, she can't have
stayed more than a minute or two because she'd gone by
the time I got there. Mrs. Mortimer was in the kitchen. I
knew she'd be hungry after such an early dinner, so I'd
got the sandwiches all ready and I made her a pot of tea. I
regret that now, as you can guess. It was probably drinking all those cups of tea that started the trouble. Still, one
can't foresee these things, can one?"

"So then what happened?"

"Well, we sat and talked for a bit while she drank it and
then Ferdy came in. He'd walked all the way home from
the Town Hall, so he was feeling thirsty too, but he had
something a little stronger; whisky, I think it was. It tells
you what a good mood Mrs. M. was in by the way she
never made any fuss about his helping himself from the
bottle, so I thought it would be quite safe to leave her in
his charge and I went up to bed. It had been quite a long
day. I heard them both come up a few minutes later and
say good night and then I must have dropped off because
I'm afraid that's the last thing I remember."

"But she was absolutely okay up to that point? No
shocks or doppelgangers along the way?"

"Nothing wrong at all. As I say, she was in better spirits
than I'd seen her for weeks. She'd been telling me all
about the play. She really enjoyed it, you know, specially
your part, she said you were splendid! Now, isn't that
nice? I meant to tell you straight away, because I knew
how pleased you'd be and, instead of that, I've gone

babbling on about my silly old self. It's your own fault, dear, for being such a sympathetic listener."

Tilly was expert in paraphrasing other people's comments in more flattering terms, so I did not allow Edna's favourable opinion to go to my head and she went on:

"Well now, I don't know about you, but all this talk of tea has given me quite a thirst. How would it be if I went down and made us both a nice cuppa?"

"Why not let me do it, Tilly? That's one department where I could make myself useful."

"Oh no, my dear, it's very sweet of you, but I know just where to lay my hands on everything, so it'll be twice as quick if I go and it'll do me good to stretch my legs a bit. You just sit here quietly and I'm sure you won't have any trouble. Don't forget, though, if you're the slightest bit nervous, or if there's any change at all, just come out on the landing and give me a call."

She folded her sewing away in her usual calm, methodical fashion, then got up and walked out of the room, her slippers making no sound on the thick pile carpet, and pausing only momentarily to glance across at the mound on the bed, as she went by.

For some while after she had left the room, I obeyed instructions, sitting perfectly still, hands folded in my lap, trying not to count the minutes until she returned. However, as time went by, a new sensation began to creep in and I gradually became possessed by a compulsion to get up and go over to the bed. At the time, I put this down to the relaxing effect of Tilly's chatter, which had soothed away my fears. In retrospect, though, I was more inclined to attribute the impulse to another influence altogether, for I could never afterwards quite rid myself of the belief that, from the first moment of our being alone together, it was the patient herself who had been willing me to get up and move closer to her.

I had detected no sound or movement, but her eyes were open and, as I approached, she fixed them on me with an agonised stare of appeal, which in fact was rather more terrifying than anything I had imagined, although strangely enough it still did not enter my head to back

away or call for help. Instead, I moved closer, bending
forward and tentatively putting out my right hand towards
hers, which had now begun to flutter out some message of
its own, and having no idea how to respond to this except
with conventional soothing gestures, as to a sick child.

The stricken look flickered momentarily into the more
familiar one of anger and impatience at my obtuseness
and, brought up sharp by this, I made a stern effort to
understand precisely what she was asking of me.

There were two bedside tables and on the one on her
right, where I was standing, were a carafe of water, two
tumblers, some bottles of pills and medicine and a jotting
pad, with a felt pen attached to it by a cord. Although
wavering and unsteady, Edna's hand left me in small doubt
as to which of these objects it was seeking and I took up
the pad, placed it on the sheet in front of her, fitted the
pen between her thumb and forefinger, then held the pad
by the two top corners to keep it steady. Throughout this
operation her eyes followed my every movement and before she began to write they met mine in a final anguished
look of appeal.

I cannot tell what Tilly's reactions may have been when
she re-entered the room and took in this scene. She
moved so quietly that my first intimation of her return was
the gentle clink of china as she set the tray down. However startled though, she must have recovered instantly
because when I turned my head she nodded and beamed
at me approvingly:

"Is this all right?" I asked softly, to which she nodded
again and smiled, setting out the cups and plates as though
this were the jolliest little tea party in the world.

"Excellent, Tessa! Couldn't be better. Carry on just as
long as you can get her to. You're a real brick!"

Her congratulations were premature, however, for when
I turned back to Edna I saw that the pen had fallen from
her hand. Her eyes were closed and a large tear was
trickling down to the corner of the rigid, misshapen mouth.
I removed one hand from the pad to signal to Tilly, who
was beside me in a flash.

"Everything all right, my dear?" she asked, addressing

Edna, who did not respond by so much as a quiver. "Just tired, I expect? Never mind, you've done very well. Try and have a little nap now and get some of that strength back. How about a sip of tea? Lift your hand if you'd like some."

The right hand remained as inert as the left and Tilly touched me gently on the shoulder, as a signal to move, at the same time replacing the pad on the table and tearing off the top page. She studied the scrawled message with an anxious frown, then, sighing and shaking her head, walked over to a little pearwood bureau, which stood in the alcove of the second window, and tucked the slip of paper into a pigeon hole.

"Bravo, Tessa!" she said, pouring out the tea. "You did very well indeed. I knew I could count on you, in spite of what you said. She has these very occasional spurts, which I feel is such a hopeful sign. As you see, though, they don't last long and it was so sensible of you to stay with her and stimulate this one as far as you could. Dr. Martin says that the longer she remains in a torpor the less chance she has of making a full recovery, so every little effort on her part is a step forward."

"Could you make any sense of what she had written?" I asked.

"No, none whatever, unfortunately; but I don't consider that so terribly important, do you? Whatever it was that came into her mind is probably forgotten now, in any case. What matters is that something did come, however fleetingly, and it roused her into a kind of awareness."

"All the same, Tilly, I should think it might help to know what it was. Before she started to write, she seemed so . . . well, terrified is the only way to describe it. If she has something on her mind which frightens her so badly, wouldn't it be a good idea to try and find out what it is?"

"My dear child, of course she's terrified! Wouldn't you be, if you woke up one morning and found yourself unable to move or speak? It's almost too appalling to think about, but my point is that it's better to have these moments of awareness, however distressing for her, than to remain in a constant stupor. That way there would be no hope at all."

It had struck me that Tilly was talking round the question, rather than answering it directly, presumably having some reason of her own for being unwilling to discuss this particular attempt by Edna to communicate, still less to show me what the attempt had resulted in. I was wrong, however, for after a moment or two of silence she put her cup down, stood up and moved in a very deliberate way to the desk. Bending down, with her back to me, as she groped in the pigeon hole, she said:

"I'd like you to see for yourself how futile it is at this stage to try and decipher these fragments of nightmares which she tries to pass on to us. This is not the first one, but it makes no more sense than the others. Not to me, that is, but you're a bright girl, so you may succeed where I've failed. Tell me what you can make of it."

She was absolutely right, as I might have known. There appeared to be three separate words on the slip of paper, one below the other and although I stared at them with all the concentration I could muster I got no further than admitting that the first and third were illegible, while the second, if it was a word, made no sense at all. They looked like this:

2

Ferdy was hoeing a flower bed beside the front door when I came out and he asked me to give him a lift into Storhampton. I think he had prepared himself for this opportunity, for he was rather too cleanly dressed for the gardening role and the bed was already immaculate.

As it happened, I had not intended to go near Storhampton, which was choked from end to end with car loads of Festival visitors and Roakes Common, where I was bound for, lay in the opposite direction. However, he was such a diffident, unassuming creature that I could not bring myself to disappoint him, although I did point out as soon as we were on our way that there were two cars languishing on the premises and, since Edna was no longer in a position to object, I wondered that he did not avail himself of one of them. To which he replied that he did not hold a driving license.

Thinking that he might have been disqualified for some reason, I said no more, but he then explained, as though it were the most natural thing in the world, that he had never owned a car, never expected to do so and had therefore never seen the necessity to take out a license.

I was somewhat stunned by this news, but it reminded me that Ferdy had always been noted for his extremely simplistic approach to life, although opinions varied as to whether this proved him to be slightly half-witted, or a lot brighter than some. He was not celebrated for his enthusiasm for the arts, either, so I asked him what had drawn him to Storhampton.

"Only the railway station," he replied. "I'm going to London."

"Oh, I see. Which train?"

"Well, the first one that comes in, I suppose," he replied, looking at me rather blankly. "So long as it's going in the right direction."

"It didn't occur to you to look one up in the timetable?"

Ferdy sighed: "I didn't know what time I should get to the station, did I?" he said, speaking slowly, as though to an idiot child, which I was rapidly beginning to feel like.

"Will you be coming back to-night?"

"More likely to-morrow or the next day. I'm not really needed here any more, you see. For the time being, at any rate."

"You mean the garden can take care of itself for a bit?"

"No, I don't mean that. Sorry, Tessa, but I thought

you'd be clued in. Tilly wanted me here to keep an eye on Edna and ward off her spook. You heard about her spook?"

"Yes."

"Well, it's not likely to be troubling her again, just at present, and even if it does there's not much I can do about it."

"On the other hand, I suppose it could still be a help to Tilly to have you around?"

"Do you honestly think so? Well, in that case . . . but how exactly? I mean, I can't drive and I'm not at all domesticated. Besides, she's got Camilla there."

"But Camilla's not very strong and I was thinking of things like lifting and lugging about and so on. Specially at night, because I imagine the nurse will only be on duty in the daytime."

"Then Tilly will just have to take her head out of the sand and call on Bernard, won't she?" Ferdy asked in his most bland voice.

It was fortunate that we had not set out to catch any particular train because, in order to reach the station, it was necessary to penetrate deep into the heart of Storhampton, then over the bridge to the opposite bank of the river, which bisected the town, and then along another half mile of the narrowest and most crowded shopping streets. We had now embarked on the first stage of this hazardous journey and, since Ferdy had not offered to get out and walk the rest of the way, which was perhaps understandable from his point of view, we were edging along at the rate of about two yards per minute. I did not complain about this, however, because we also seemed to be edging towards something else.

"You are implying that Bernard spends his nights at Farndale?"

"Yes, the only reason I know about it is that they got locked out one night, which caused a right old fuss. Camilla had lost the key, or she'd given it to Bernard and he'd lost it, I can't remember now. Anyway, Tilly explained to me that it was something to do with Camilla using his car. He can bring her home at night and then she drives him to the office in the morning and takes the car on."

"Honestly, Ferdy!"

"I know, comical isn't it? But it all comes from Camilla being so keen to toe the line and keep in with my step-mother. I can't tell you why, but there it is, she's always been like that. And of course Edna would have been down on them like a ton of bricks if she'd found out there was this immorality going on under her roof. And there's Tilly keeping her conscience quiet by going around pretending it's all just a matter of convenience, which I suppose it is, in a way. Anyway, they won't need to cover up now and if Bernard does have to lend a hand in the night it won't matter because, as far as I can make out, even if Edna did recognise him, she wouldn't know if it was Saturday or Christmas Eve."

"Was Bernard staying there last night?"

"Suppose so. Why? Why not, I mean?"

He was groping in his pockets and answering in an abstracted way, so I said:

"Nothing much. I was only thinking that it now turns out that there were probably no less than four people within yards of Edna when she came crashing down on the landing and yet none of them heard her, or knew a thing about it. Doesn't that strike you as odd?"

"I suppose so. No, not particularly."

"What on earth are you looking for, Ferdy?"

"Money. Thought I'd got some with me, but I must have left it behind. It doesn't matter."

"It must matter. How will you buy a ticket to London without any money?"

"Oh, that's okay, they'll always take a cheque. It's just that I'm out of fags."

So when I finally drove away from the station the balance sheet looked like this: one hour late getting home and one pound poorer; and on the credit side: one more petty little deceit of Camilla's to add to the collection. It hardly seemed worth the outlay.

CHAPTER TEN

•

Mindful of the gnawing, insatiable vanity of the creative writer, I was careful to give Toby a full, verbatim report of all the flattering words which had been poured out in praise of his play, before filling him in with recent events at Farndale House. Even the mellow mood which this spade work engendered, however, did not prompt him to treat them very seriously. He had always detested Edna and my description of her present unhappy plight hardly moved him at all.

"I didn't expect you to burst into tears," I complained, "but I did hope you would agree with me that it is all distinctly fishy."

"What is?"

"Well, four people, four mark you, all with their faculties properly tuned up, and not one of them saw or heard a thing."

"How do you know? One of them may have seen and heard a great deal and decided it was all for the best. I know I should have."

"No, you wouldn't, Toby, not even you. Certain reflexes take over in a crisis of that kind and, however much one may dislike a person, one doesn't just step over the corpse and leave it on the bathroom floor."

"Then what are we arguing about? Since it has been established that no such reflexes were functioning last

54

night, it must follow that none of the four did see or hear anything. It may be exceptional, but it is not fishy."

"Except that they might not have functioned in the case of someone who saw and heard exactly what he was expecting."

"Oh, I'm with you now, with you all the way. You think this seizure was contrived by one of them? Well, that wouldn't surprise me at all, but you're out of luck, aren't you?"

"Am I?"

"Certainly, you are, because if the old harridan should die it will inevitably be attributed to natural causes; which means that no one is going to ask for your help in a lovely murder investigation."

"There is such a thing, Toby, as seeking out the truth for its own sake."

"So I've heard, but I'm afraid you won't get very far with that either. They're a very well organised little herd at Farndale, with Tilly running round like a zealous sheep-dog whenever they show signs of straying. You wouldn't get a foot in there. Incidentally, I presume you believe one of them has been impersonating Edna's doppelganger literally in order to scare her to death?"

"I regard it as a possibility."

"So perhaps you have already decided which one?"

"No, not yet, but most of my money is on her sister, Alice. After all, she does start with the advantage of having some physical resemblance to the victim. It would certainly have been a lot easier for her than anyone else."

"Unfortunately, that doesn't make it any more probable. She happens to be the only one of them who is not obliged to dance attendance on Edna and put up with her mean-ness and bad temper. Why should she bother with such pranks?"

"Well, I can't tell you why, Toby, but I think that's how it may have started: as a malicious prank. Apparently, she's always been jealous of Edna, who never missed an opportunity to snub and humiliate her. It must have ran-kled and now that she's retired and hard up, stripped of all her matronly power, as you might say, it must be even more irritating to think of her beastly sister lapped in luxury and not lifting a finger. But there's another thing, which makes an even more damning case against Alice, that I haven't mentioned yet."

"I thought there must be."

"Tilly told me that when she rang her up this morning, to pass on the sad news, Alice immediately offered her professional services."

"What's guilt laden about that? Personally, I consider it rather magnanimous. And since she's a trained nurse, with time on her hands, what more natural?"

"But Toby, you know as well as I do that if Edna woke up and found Alice bending over her with the hypodermic it would not only delay her recovery, but probably precipitate her death. Tilly told me she had to tie herself in knots to head Alice off. She explained why more or less as I have, but I expect she had an extra reason too."

"And what would that be?"

"Don't you see that if it had occurred to her that Alice had been running round impersonating her sister, this would be a marvellous way to insinuate herself into the household and have another go? Captive audience, already very groggy, and Edna's entire wardrobe there for her to choose from."

"Yes, but that would take it out of the category of malicious prank. That really would be intent to murder."

"And for all we know, Alice has a more sinister motive than appears. If so, I wouldn't put anything past her and neither, I suspect, would Tilly."

"So there you are! Tilly is right up alongside, if not one jump ahead of you, and she'll never let any cat out of her old knitting bag."

"Aren't you forgetting something, Toby?"

"Am I? I do seem to forget most things. What is it this time?"

"Edna herself may be the one to tell us. She obviously has something very pressing on her mind and, if she only regained part of her faculties, she might be able to write down a legible message. Furthermore, that is just as likely to happen when the nurse is there as at any other time, in which case Tilly would be powerless to conceal it."

"I suppose so, but I wouldn't have thought the risk was enormous. Didn't you tell me her last effort made no sense whatever?"

"I wrote it down for you," I said, taking a piece of paper from my bag, "just in case your keen mind detects some hidden meaning."

It looked at first as though it did, for, having scrutinised it briefly, he handed it back to me, saying:

"That's easy, no trouble at all. It says 'IOU one pound, love Ferdy'."

"Oh sorry, that's the wrong side. The silly fellow insisted on making it what he called official, so when he'd gone I used the back of his IOU to copy out Edna's squiggles, as exactly as I could remember them."

This time there was a longer interval before Toby looked up and then he said:

"After all, my keen mind is no more use than a wet flannel. I can only begin to make out one of the words and, by a long stretch of the imagination, it might be construed as 'ell'. Perhaps she was trying to say: 'I gave them an inch and they took an el'. That would be rather her style. But no wonder old Tilly saw no harm in showing it to you! Even you would be hard pressed to read anything between those lines."

He was about to crush the piece of paper into a ball, but I snatched it from him protesting loudly:

"Don't do that! Ferdy was so fussy about giving it to me that, for all I know, he may expect me to return it to him when he pays me back."

"In that case, I should advise you to put it in the bank. You could well be a bed-ridden old lady yourself before that day comes."

CHAPTER ELEVEN

•

An upstairs restaurant in one of the riverside pubs was making a good thing out of Three Course After Theatre Suppers and Special Matinee Luncheons. I make it a rule never to eat lunch before a matinee, special or otherwise, but on the day after my visit to Farndale we had only an evening performance and when Helena Plowman telephoned in the morning and invited me to join her in the dining room of the Jolly Angler I accepted at once.

I had scarcely known Helena until the Festival set our paths crossing and had never felt this left any gaping blank in my life, but she had said that she wished to ask my advice on a confidential matter, which was too much to resist; and the shaming part of it was that I could not quite repress the sneaking hope that Camilla was turning out to be totally inadequate for the job and that the advice Helena sought was in how to give her the graceful sack. I felt more ashamed than ever when this proved to be true.

"Apart from being contemporaries, you two have always been such close friends," Helena said, rubbing salt in the wound, then wiping it off again by adding: "And, since it was largely thanks to you that we've been saddled with her, I thought you might be able to give me some guidelines."

I had been studying her, in her cool, uncrushed toffee coloured shirtwaister, while she put the waiter through an inquisition on the ingredients of the Special Lunch and had come to the conclusion that she had changed very little since the days when, with a single word or look, she had struck terror into the unruly elements at the children's parties. She was a woman who went to infinite pains to get the smallest details right, as the present instance proved, and this near-obsession applied to every aspect of her life. She always had the right flowers in the right vase, on the most polished of Sheraton tables; always meticulously checked, repeated and retained for ever the name of a stranger on being introduced, and was always immaculately dressed in the most suitable clothes for every occasion. Apart from a rather daunting lack of humour and something chilly and anaemic in her appearance, the principal flaw in all this studied perfection was that her pale blue eyes were set slightly too close together, which was probably how Bernard came by his shifty look.

However, there were some more nebulous faults too, to tarnish the image. For some reason, her poise and self-assurance, far from transmitting itself to others, created a barrier of unease. It was as though she were forever playing a part which Nature had not written for her and that deep within herself she was still worried about fluffing her lines. This impression of being slightly at odds with herself had sometimes caused me to wonder whether she suffered from a total lack of the vulgar streak, or whether it was there all right and had only been partially repressed, so that she was always afraid it would bob up some day and catch her unawares.

I was not unique in having been repelled on occasions by this enigmatic quality and various stories and rumours had been dragged out to account for it. One was that in her early youth she had been engaged to the heir of a rich and noble family, that the wedding had been cancelled at the last minute, in somewhat dubious circumstances, as a result of which she had been bundled up the aisle with a second-rate country solicitor, an humiliation from which she had never wholly recovered. Another favourite was that her marriage to Robert Plowman had been disappointing and unsatisfactory, causing her to project her worldly ambitions on to Bernard, who was destined in her

eyes to achieve all the glories she had missed and who had
upset these schemes by turning out to be a weak and
undistinguished boy, very much like his father.

"What's gone wrong?" I asked, in response to her opening statement. "I understood Camilla was doing so well."

"I don't know where you got that idea! She got by, so
long as Debbie Fox was in charge and able to chivvy her,
but it's a different story now. By the most maddening
stroke of bad luck, poor Debbie has had a miscarriage and
has had to retire from the fray. The Committee really had
no choice but to hand things over to Camilla. We thought
she'd have got the hang of it by then, but we couldn't have
been more mistaken, and what's much worse is that she
seems to have lost interest. Everyone is entitled to make
mistakes from time to time, but it's this attitude of apathy
and *laissez-faire* which is so trying. She's simply not pulling her weight."

"You don't think it's just that she's worried over this
business with her grandmother?"

"Yes, no doubt, that could have something to do with
it," Helena said, prodding her melon in a suspicious way.
"And, goodness knows, I don't want to be hard on the girl.
I know things must be difficult and I admire her for giving
up her London job to spend more time down here. I just
wish I could find the right way to ease her out, without
hurting her feelings. Unfortunately, I'm the very last person for that, although I don't feel that it gives me an
excuse to shirk it."

"Oh really? I should have thought you were expert at
striking the tactful note?"

"My dear girl, do use your head! As her prospective
mother-in-law, I am naturally suspect. So much so that it
never occurred to her to apply to me in the first place, if
you remember?"

"Well, couldn't you just say that now the Festival is on
its feet, so to speak, you're scrapping that department
altogether?"

"Which just shows how very little you know about all
the hard work that goes on behind the scenes! Even
Camilla would see through that! The fact is that keeping

the press happy is absolutely vital at this stage. My dear, do you realise it was purely by accident that I discovered that not a single Oxford or Dedley paper had been sent tickets to cover your opening performance? Fortunately, Tara managed to straighten it out in the nick of time, but it could have been a fiasco. Heaven knows what our dear impresario, Mr. David Winter, would have had to say about it!"

Leaving him out of it, I was pretty badly shocked myself: "Well, I'll be blowed! How did Camilla talk her way out of that one?"

"Quite unrepentant. Said she'd arranged with the box office for anyone with a press card to be given complimentary tickets, but I ask you, Tessa! What's the good of that? You have to woo these people, you can't expect them to make the running. And we have our Japanese Film Week coming up to-morrow," Helena added thoughtfully. "People may not actually be fighting to get in, even if it does get a decent write-up and I'm just keeping my fingers crossed that our Camilla won't have fallen down on that one, too."

"Still, however lousy a job she's doing, you're not going to find it easy to replace her at this stage?"

"On the contrary, Tara's perfectly willing to take over and she'd do a first class job, no question of that."

"Then why . . . ?"

"Oh, she had far too much on her plate during the preparatory period. No one could believe what that woman takes on! But now that we're off the ground, so to speak, the pressures are off too, and she could handle the press side without turning a hair. Naturally, though, she insists on having a clear field, and I don't think Camilla would take kindly to having someone else in authority, so the problem is how to shift her without hurting her feelings or setting up an extra hostility towards myself. That's where I was looking to you for some advice. You've hardly touched your fish! Is there anything wrong with it?"

The only truthful answer was that it tasted as though the chef had cooked it in the bag and then thrown all but the bag away, so I took refuge in Camilla's trick of substituting a vapid smile for the spoken word, before returning to the point of discussion:

"If you want an honest opinion, Helena, I'd say you haven't much to worry about. A face saver is all you need and there won't be any danger of hurting her feelings. Explain that her exceptional talents will henceforth be needed for keeping a check on the car stickers and you'll be home and dry."

"Indeed?" Helena asked snootily. "You do surprise me! One had always thought of her as a particularly sensitive young woman. Hyper-sensitive, one might almost say."

"I know one might, but that's when her own feelings are concerned, and that's not the case here. This job was simply the means to an end."

"Good heavens!" Helena said, looking quite scandalised by such heresy. "To what end, pray?"

"Well, you see, when Mrs. Mortimer had her visitation from the spirit world, or whatever it was that caused the first attack . . ."

"I beg your pardon?" Helena interrupted, frowning so heavily that it gave her a slight squint. "What's all this talk of spirits?"

"Oh, you know, this mysterious apparition that's been bobbing up during the past two or three weeks. No one is sure whether Mrs. Mortimer has imagined it, but each of her bad spells has been brought on by seeing someone who was so nearly her own double that she concluded she'd died and was looking at herself from another world. Bernard must have told you about it?"

"I assure you he hasn't."

"Honestly? How very strange! We seem to have been talking about nothing else for weeks; but I suppose he doesn't take it very seriously."

"And also you must remember that I've had rather a lot on my plate recently," she reminded me, looking self-righteous about it, as people are apt to do when they have missed out on a sizzling bit of gossip. "Besides, Bernard has never confided in us very much. However, go on with what you were saying about Camilla."

"Oh, simply that she's hooked on the idea that she has

some kind of obligation to stick around during this rather alarming phase, but not in such a way that she'd be tied to the house the whole time. Furthermore, I think that was also the last thing Tilly wanted, so it suited all parties for Camilla to play the dutiful grand-daughter, with none of the boredom the role would normally have entailed. Mind you, that's only my personal opinion."

"And a depressingly cynical one, if I may say so! However, you may be right and I certainly hope you are, because it will make my task a lot easier. I think I've just time for coffee, if you'd like some?"

Having unburdened herself and been granted such an acceptable solution, she unbent quite a lot while we drank our coffee, even stooping so low as to press for details about Edna's hallucinations and declaring herself to be quite as mystified as the rest of us when she had heard the full story.

"Of course, she is apt to dramatise even the most ordinary events, but frankly I wouldn't have thought she had the imagination to invent a tale like this."

"Which is the view that most people take."

"It's odd really," Helena mused, squinting into her cup. "If one didn't know better, it would be so easy to assume that she and Camilla were blood relations. They have so much in common. Some of the resemblances are quite remarkable."

"Not having their feet quite on the ground, for instance?"

"I wouldn't have put it as strongly as that," Helena replied, obviously regarding this as a terrible condemnation. "But, without wishing to be unkind, you must know what I mean? This trick of saying whatever comes into their heads, in order to justify themselves in some way?"

"Yes, I expect it's catching. Were you surprised when she and Bernard got engaged?"

"I must confess I was," Helena said, grimacing slightly as she put her cup down. "Very much surprised, as it happens. Not that I've anything against Camilla, you understand, but Robert and I both thought Bernard and Fiona Batterby would make a match of it. You know her, I expect?"

I shook my head.

"The Tivertons' eldest girl; an absolute poppet and she and Bernard have been chums since they were in their teens. Still, it can't have been serious, I suppose, because, out of the blue, he tells us that he's going to marry Camilla."

"A touch of the rebounds, perhaps?"

"Couldn't say, my dear. One has learnt not to ask questions. I'm sure Camilla will make a splendid wife, but they certainly don't behave like engaged couples used to in my day."

"More like brother and sister, you mean?"

"Not exactly, no. That wouldn't bother me so much because I think a good many young people adopt that kind of pose nowadays. A form of self-consciousness, perhaps, or something to do with the clothes they wear, but my pair aren't like that at all. I don't know how I can explain it to you, but they're more like two people collaborating in some business arrangement. While the deal is going through they live entirely in each other's pockets, even take pleasure in doing so, and yet somehow you know instinctively that once their business has been concluded they'll both move on to new enterprises and scarcely give a thought to each other ever again. Oh well, it's just their way, I suppose and probably I'm out of touch with modern customs. You obviously haven't the faintest idea what I'm driving at, if that gawpy look is anything to go by."

I did not disillusion her, but in fact my gaping, half-witted expression was due not to want of comprehension, but to the simple wonder of dear old, conventional Helena having come up with an analysis which so perfectly matched my own, having reached it moreover from a directly opposite approach.

CHAPTER TWELVE

•

1

Toby had underestimated Ferdy in one respect, for he repayed the borrowed pound as soon as he returned from London on Thursday evening. In fact, he came straight from the railway station to the Methodist Chapel, arriving there just after the final curtain. I must have looked stunned when he handed over the money, for he said soothingly:

"It's okay; it's been a profitable day."

"Oh, that's good. Were you working?"

"Sort of. I've been at Lingfield."

"Oh, I see! Well, congratulations! Don't you find it a drag, though, Ferdy, trailing round to all these race meetings without a car?"

"Not a bit. Much less trouble to go by train. They mostly run right up to the course and they're timed to coincide with the first and last races."

"Really? That must be convenient. I didn't know."

"Well, don't spread it around, or they'll start closing down the lines."

"In the meantime, how will you get home tonight? There's no train service to Farndale."

"Well, I can always walk, but as a matter of fact I was hoping to cadge a lift from you," he replied, with his innocent smile, causing me to wonder whether, after all, there had been some method in the madness of repaying the loan.

"Okay, I suppose it wouldn't kill me, but you'll have to wait outside while I change. It'll take me ten minutes."

"Right. I'll nip across to the pub. See you outside."

Two minutes later there was a knock on the door and he was back:

"Terribly sorry, Tessa, but I'm right out. Think you could lend me thirty pence for a beer?"

"Any news?" he enquired, as we drove out of Storhampton. "How's my old step-ma doing?"

"I haven't had an up-to-date bulletin," I told him. "There hasn't been time for anything to-day, with two performances to get through, but I met Camilla on her rounds yesterday and she said there hadn't been any noticeable improvement. They were rather depressed about it."

"Yes, I'd got as far as that. I spoke to Tilly on the telephone last night and she sounded slightly demented. Kept burbling on about how there hadn't been any more messages. I never found out what she meant by that because the pips went and I'd used up all my change."

"Presumably, she meant that Edna hadn't made another attempt to write anything down."

"Oh, really? How could she do that, though? I thought she was paralysed?"

"Only on one side. She's able to use her right hand a little and when I was there, and also once or twice before that, she'd tried to write some sort of message on the pad they keep by her bed. You mean, you didn't know about that?"

"No, but there's no reason why I should. They wouldn't have thought it worth bothering to tell me."

He made this statement with complete matter-of-factness as though recognising the validity of it, so I did not dispute it either and after a pause for thought he said:

"What kind of stuff was she writing then? About feeling thirsty, things like that?"

"No, nothing so coherent. Just wavery squiggles is all she's managed so far."

There was another silence and then Ferdy said gravely:
"That's rough, really rough. Don't you agree? Must be

frustrating for her, I mean. Well, thanks for the lift, Tessa. You've saved my life all over again. You can drop me at the gate, if you like."

"No, it's okay. I've got to turn somewhere, so I may as well deliver you to your door."

He was a great one for bobbing up again after the farewells were over and this time he came scooting out of the house, waving his arms in the air, as I was backing up for the second time on the awkward shaped gravel patch in front of the house. I switched off the engine and he cantered over to the car.

"Tilly wants you to come in," he explained. "That is, if you can spare a few more minutes?"

"Oh, sure! Anything wrong?"

"Plenty. Edna is dead and Camilla's having hysterics."

2

"Thank heavens you're still up," I said, when I crawled home more than an hour later.

"I am only up because I had to come down," Toby informed me crossly. "Robin keeps ringing up. I have just put the receiver down for the second time since I went to bed."

"I'm always telling you you ought to have an extension in your room. You're as bad as old Benjamin Mortimer. Is Robin all right?"

"Fair to middling. Slightly anoyed to find you still out at one in the morning. He hopes you're not mixed up in something."

"His hopes will be dashed. I am mixed up in something."

"You look as though you were. You must tell me all about it in the morning."

"Not now?"

"No, in the morning."

"Edna's dead."

"Oh, good!" he said, continuing his relentless ascent to his room.

There was nothing to be done with him in that mood

and I followed his example and went to my bedroom. Not
to sleep, however, because I had also done Ferdy a slight
injustice and, while checking through my diary for the
morning's first appointment, I came across his IOU, which
he had not asked me to return. Having crossed out £1 and
substituted 30p, I turned it over for a last look at the
scrawls on the back and something struck me which I had
not noticed before. This was hardly surprising, for I was
now looking at it upside down; or rather, as my jaded
brain eventually grasped, I could equally well be seeing it
the right way up for the very first time. The chances were
about even because it was now the first line which was
faintly legible, whereas the other two were meaningless.

What kept me awake long after I had gone to bed and
switched off the light was the endless and futile struggle to
decide whether Edna's last message had really contained
the word, or part word "ell", or the beginning of the word
"will" and, if the latter, whether Tilly's initial presentation
of it had been by accident or design.

3

"Very well, you may tell me about it now, if you insist,"
Toby said, when he had fortified himself with eggs and
coffee. "I won't suggest that you begin at the beginning
because that might be rather dull, and also it would take
far too long. Pick out some of the highlights. How, for
example, did you come to be there at all at that time of
night?"

When I had explained this, he asked:

"Why was Camilla having hysterics?"

"Because it was all her fault that Edna had died. Or so
she said. Even when she'd calmed down a bit, she still
managed to make a big production of it. Insisted on going
alone to Edna's room, to ask forgiveness and say her last
goodbyes in private. Did you ever hear of such affected
nonsense?"

"No, but I congratulate you! That's what I call a high-
light. More than one, in fact."

"Of low candle power, however, because she didn't confess to having waltzed around as a phantom, dressed up in granny's mink. What it boiled down to was a small case of neglect on her part."

"How small?"

"Well, you see, the nurse went off duty at six and then Tilly took over until nine. They'd arranged that after that Camilla and Bernard should share the watch until midnight, either together or in turns. Tilly was going to be on duty for the rest of the night. They'd rigged up a camp bed for her, so that at least she could lie down, but you can see that, as usual, she was taking the lion's share, and that's why Camilla feels so rotten about letting her down. Or so she says."

"You don't seem to place much reliance on the poor girl's word."

"Well, hers is the line which anyone would be well advised to take if their conscience was troubling them, and it might be true and it might not. She's got Bernard to back her up in parts of her story, but I don't set much store by that, do you?"

"None whatever, but I'm regretting that I didn't ask you to start at the beginning, after all. It is now dawning on me that, as well as being rather confusing, this way may take even longer."

"It began at nine o'clock last night, when Camilla reported for duty. She and Bernard had dined together and Tilly had hers on a tray. Then Bernard slunk off to watch a television programme, telling Camilla that he'd be up fairly soon to keep her company. There'd been no change in Edna's condition and no flashes of awareness, so it was just a matter of sweating it out during each shift. Tilly wasn't in the mood for television, so she went to her room to write letters, and poor Camilla naturally got very bored all on her own and forbidden even to read because of having to keep the room in darkness; and what with all that torture and also being so absolutely exhausted after her hard day's work, she pretty soon fell asleep."

"Or so she says?"

"Or so she says. She also says that she woke up in a

fearful fright, absolutely convinced that there was a third person in the room. As a matter of fact, I've often had that sensation myself, haven't you? Camilla says it was so strong this time that it took her a while to snap out of it and get herself together again. When she'd done so, she went over to the bed, but there seemed to be nothing going on there, and it was while she was groping her way back to her chair that she realised the door was shut and that really threw her."

"Oh, do tell me why?"

"Well, it's always left open, you see; for several reasons, actually. One is that it's a creaky old door which makes a hell of a noise when you open it, another that it makes it easier for anyone who's looking after the patient to call for help in an emergency, but I think the main one is that it does provide a little indirect light from the landing, but not enough to upset Edna."

"I see; so what did Camilla do next?"

"She opened the door and went out on to the landing, but there was no one there, so she concluded the draught must have blown it shut. She knew she wasn't supposed to leave her post for an instant, but, having gone so far, she simply couldn't resist the impulse to tell Bernard about her nasty fright, only unfortunately that resulted in her getting a much worse one. When she reached the top of the stairs she distinctly heard the click of the front door."

"Or so she says?"

"Quite so. It gets more bizarre by the minute, doesn't it? She knew it couldn't have been Bernard going out because she could hear the television going, although what that's supposed to prove I really couldn't say."

"It could have been Tilly, I daresay; making a trip down to the pillar box with all those letters?"

"No, because Tilly was having a bath. Camilla could hear the water running. That bit, at least, was true because it was the element which added so much to the chaos and mayhem when the hysterics began; Tilly trying to calm her down, I mean, while dripping wet and wrapped in a bath towel."

"Am I to understand that Camilla went into hysterics because her governess was having a bath?"

"No, on the contrary, that seems to have cheered her up a lot; everything nice and normal again. So much so that she began to think the rest of it had been part of a dream and that it was probably high time she returned to her charge, before anyone discovered her skipping about on the landing."

"But too late? The patient had been gathered, I take it?"

"Correct!"

"Very distressing, I can see that, but was there really any need for such violent reaction? They must all have been expecting it?"

"Well, apparently, it wasn't one of those nice gentle deaths; sweet old lady slipping away with an expression of deep peace, or anything of that kind. This one had her eyes wide open and her mouth stretched into a kind of snarl. So it can't have been very pleasant for the poor girl, but if you ask me she was laying it on a bit strong mainly to escape the awkward questions. After all, if someone is bawling and moaning that it's all their fault, even if you're inclined to agree and half suspect her of telling a bucketful of lies, it usually ends with patting her on the head and insisting that she has nothing to reproach herself with. At any rate, that was certainly Tilly's reaction."

"Whereas you, lacking such a charitable nature, question whether she fell asleep at all? You think it more in character for her and Bernard to have held a pillow over Edna's head?"

"God knows, Toby, and even if He were to tell us, it wouldn't help much. How right you were to warn me that if there were any sharp practice involved in this one there would never be a hope of proving it, far less of finding out who was responsible."

"To which, if I remember, you retorted with some rather high flown sentiments about beauty being truth, truth beauty."

"There now! Did I really? I never knew I had such stuff

in me. Well, perhaps I should make an effort to live up to it. After all, the story isn't finished yet, is it?"

"Isn't it?"

"Certainly not. We still have to find out what becomes of all the money. Who can say what new fields may be opened up for us when we learn about Edna's will?"

CHAPTER THIRTEEN

•

It was unremarkable in every way except one. Every moral and family obligation had been faithfully discharged, an exactly suitable sum bequeathed to the most respectable of local and national charities, and the single surprise lay in its being so just and fair, which was something which no one who knew her would ever have looked for in Edna.

The essence of the matter was that Tilly and Alice each received a lump sum, Alice getting an added bonus in the form of jewellery and personal belongings, the residue being divided equally between Ferdy and Camilla.

This much was known to everyone in the Mortimer circle within forty-eight hours, but I heard the details a day or two later from Vi and Marge, when I visited them at the Art Exhibition, which was housed in the Town Hall basement. We were by then half way through the second week of the Festival and of the ninety or so paintings and sculptures on display less than a third had been sold. Most of the remainder were to be returned to their owners, but a handful of the artists concerned had consented to their works being auctioned off on the closing day, from which they were to receive ten per cent of the price, the rest going into the Festival kitty. Out of this lot, one painting had been set aside for first prize in a raffle, inevitably organised and operated by Vi and Marge, and they had invited me to attend the closing ceremony, when I was to pick a ticket from the drum and, after a hushed pause, hand the prize over to the lucky winner.

It had not struck me as being a particularly complicated or demanding task, but Tara Goodchild, who was never one to over-estimate other people's abilities, had considered it desirable that I should be primed and rehearsed in advance.

She was sitting between them when I arrived, behind a trestle table which was set out, in rather optimistic fashion with books of tickets and large tin cash boxes, and she was wearing a flimsy, washed out mauve and green sari, under a thick brown, handknitted cardigan. It was both dank and sombre in these nether regions and she had managed to reflect the prevailing atmosphere to perfection.

The prize painting was on an easel beside the table. It was a view of the river from Storhampton bridge, in water colour, and I was about to remark that, far from being a lucky winner, only a lunatic would have invested the price of a single ticket in such a monstrosity, when it occurred to me just in time that it had most likely been selected for the honour by Tara herself, if not indeed executed by her. The river was depicted as muddy grey, all the trees a limp and pallid green and the church steeple sticking up through the middle of them was dark brown, the whole effect being extremely fuzzy and depressing.

Needless to say, business was not brisk and they offered me some coffee, to fortify me for the run-through of the prize giving routine. I could not imagine where it would come from, so accepted out of curiosity, whereupon Tara dived into a shopping basket and brought out four cardboard cups, a jar of instant coffee, milk, sugar, and spoons and a thermos of hot water, all proof of her amazing, highly praised efficiency. She also handed me my speech of congratulation to the winning entrant.

As I had expected, it consisted of the conventional trite phrases, with a couple of feeble jokes thrown in, but there was one allusion in it which mystified me:

"Who is this celebrated local artist, A. Dilloway, to whom we express our sincere thanks for this most generous gift?" I enquired. "I hever heard of him in my life."

"Oh yes, you have," Marge said, "and it's not a him, it's a her."

"Oh? Still doesn't help, I'm afraid."

"Well, think of all the people you've been hearing about lately whose names begin with A."

I struggled to do so, but could only produce one:

"You wouldn't be referring to Edna's sister, Alice?"

"Right first time!"

"You don't tell me! I never heard her surname before; and I didn't know she was . . . artistic."

"Well, you know now," Marge said with a heavy wink. "And, of course, these days she can afford to give her wares away to charity, frames and all."

I stood up to get a better view of the painting, which turned out to be more hideous still at close quarters. I gazed at it in mute horror, until Tara said:

"Do you admire this picture so much then?"

"What? Oh well, you know, I mean, it's unusual, isn't it?"

"No, not at all, not in the least; purely representational. Original is what you are meaning to say, perhaps?"

"Yes, perhaps."

"Well, I am afraid we cannot sell you any tickets for it. We should be in hot water if you were to pull out your own number."

"And I have a horrid feeling I might. Is there some more of her work on display?"

Tara shook her head: "No, that is the only one, so you are scotched again. But still, if you're interested, I have one or two at home. Why not come and have a cup of tea one day and see them?"

"Yes, I'd like to very much. When can I come?"

"To-morrow, if you like. My elder daughter will be at home then. She is bursting to meet you."

"That's very kind of you. I have a matinee to-morrow, so I couldn't be there before five. Would that be too late?"

"No, certainly not, but you have reminded me that I also have an appointment this afternoon at five o'clock, so now I shall love you and leave you," Tara said, gathering up her shopping basket, plus a leather bag the size of a junior portmanteau, and clumping off in her heavy brown shoes.

"May one ask what that was all about?" Vi enquired when she had gone. "You can't really be keen to see more of those dreadful paintings?"

"No, but I feel curious about Alice, you see. I don't know her at all. Someone pointed her out to me once, but that's as near as I've got to meeting her."

"It's as near as most people would want to get," Marge remarked.

"And why this curiosity?"

"Oh well, I suppose because she's a sort of mystery woman, in her small way," I explained, making it up as I went along. "I mean, no one has a good word for her, so far as I can make out and yet she must have some admirable qualities to have risen to be Matron of a hospital, wouldn't you say? And now she turns out to be an artist as well. I do think people who paint must have something special about them, don't you agree?"

All this was sheer rubbish, of course, but the best I could do on the spur of the moment, not feeling inclined to confess that my interest in Alice Dilloway lay principally in trying to find out whether she had frightened her sister to death.

"Well, she's special in another way now," Marge said. "I daresay we shall be seeing quite a different Alice in future. To go from rags to riches overnight must change people's outlook, particularly if they were not expecting it."

"How do you know she wasn't expecting it?"

"Helena told me. Vi thinks it was rather indiscreet of her, but personally I can't see that it matters."

"And how does Helena know?"

"Through Robert, her husband, of course. He acted for both of them. Drew up their wills and did the conveyancing for this little semi-detached Alice has moved into. He told Helena that Alice never had the slightest idea that she had expectations, or might one day be able to afford a better sort of house."

"Although, presumably, if she had known in theory, it

wouldn't have made any difference? There must have been a good chance that the expectations would never be realised. They were about the same age, weren't they?"

"No, Alice is a year or two younger. Besides, she's been forced by necessity to lead an austere and healthy life, whereas Edna's was one long self-indulgence. It is not at all surprising that Alice has outlived her."

"So how much will she get for her pains?"

"Fifty thousand, so we're told."

"Coo! As much as that? And the same for Tilly?"

"So they say. Ferdy and Camilla come off even better, of course."

"What's their share?"

Vi tried to intervene:

"How would it be, Tessa, if you were to take a couple of these books with you? You might unload a few on Toby, so long as you keep fairly vague about the prize, and I expect you'll be able to flog some to your friends in the theatre. But mind you don't forget to write their names clearly on the counterfoils. That's most important."

"Oh, if you say so," I replied without enthusiasm.

Luckily, Marge was on my side:

"I really can't see what harm there is in telling her, Vi. It will all be published in *The Times* eventually; or she could find out for herself by going to Somerset House."

"So save me the bother," I suggested. "How much are Ferdy and Camilla likely to collect?"

"Robert told Helena that after tax and other deductibles the estate will come out at anything up to three hundred thousand, so you can work it out for yourself."

"I'm too dizzy to cope with even such a simple sum as that."

"And you're not the only one, I daresay. Ferdy and Camilla must be feeling a bit dazed too. I know I would be."

"In fact," Marge added thoughtfully, "you could say that if the poor woman had to die she chose the best moment to do it."

"Oh, could you?" I asked, the dizziness passing in a flash. "Why's that?"

"Oh well, you know how she was continually changing her will, or threatening to? No, perhaps you don't, but you won't be surprised to hear that it was one of her favourite pastimes. A lovely way of bringing her entourage to heel when they showed an inclination to stray. If I were being really unkind, which thank God I'm not, I should guess that this was what chiefly inspired Camilla to dig herself in at Farndale after Edna had her first attack. She may have felt it wasn't the moment for taking chances."

"And if you were being doubly unkind, which thank God you never are," Vi remarked, "you could say exactly the same of Ferdy. For all his sweet and feckless ways, he certainly jumped to it when the old lady started to go downhill."

"You couldn't say it of Alice or Tilly though," I pointed out. "Seeing that Alice is reputed not to have known she was in the running; and one couldn't impute such base motives to Tilly."

"Perhaps not," Marge agreed placidly, "though it's amazing what the smell of fifty thousand can do to the most upright character and presumably she had some incentive for putting up with Edna so nobly for all those years. Well, personally, I do thank God I'm not unkind and I'm glad it's turned out like this. On the whole, I'd say they'd earned their luck and it must be such a comfort to them to know how well they all behaved at the end."

CHAPTER FOURTEEN

•

Back at the Chapel again for the evening performance, I found an envelope on my dressing table addressed simply to TESSA in large capitals. Inside were three coins and a note from Ferdy, inviting me to meet him for a drink after the show, at the Jolly Angler. I interpreted this as merely a civil gesture on his part, assuming that he would not care whether I turned up or not, but since there is something anti-climactic about going straight home to bed when the curtain comes down and it is quite pleasant to indulge in some gentle unwinding in between, I took him at his word.

However, it soon became clear that I had not been invited there to hear some perfunctory compliments on my lovely performance, for Ferdy had no sooner bought a beer for himself, a brandy and soda for me, borrowed the money to pay for both and carried them over to the quietest corner of the saloon bar than he announced that he wished to obtain my advice on a tricky and delicate subject.

Experience having taught me that problems in this category invariably spring from financial roots and that he was hoping to borrow a little something to tide him over until he got his hands on a hundred thousand pounds, I explained that I was a bit short myself until the end of the week, but was willing to give him a lift home if that would solve the immediate difficulty.

Surprisingly, this offer provoked a good deal of merriment and when he had finished giggling over it, he announced that the trouble lay not in how to acquire money, but, on the contrary, how to get rid of it without rocking the boat.

"You wouldn't be referring to your inheritance, by any chance?"

"That's right," he agreed, after a glance to left and right, as though to make sure we would not be overheard. "Clever of you to guess!"

"And you want to get rid of it? Give it away, you mean?"

"No, not exactly. The trouble is, I'm not even sure it's mine to give. What bothers me, you see, Tessa, is that I don't believe I'm strictly entitled to it."

"Why not? The will's perfectly valid, isn't it?"

"Yes, it's not that."

"What then?"

He remained silent for a minute or two, slowly drinking his beer and frowning, so that I thought his mind had begun to wander from the point, until he said:

"Look, Tessa, would it be okay to go and sit in your car while we talk? This place is going to close down soon and it's rather a long story."

"All right," I agreed, "but we can do better than that. I've got two shows tomorrow, so I don't want to stay up late. I'll drive you home and you can tell me as we go along."

As things turned out, there was a bit of just sitting and talking, after all, although this took place outside the gate of Farndale House, for it really was a long story and only half told by the end of the three mile drive. This was partly due to his being a slow speaker, who took a long while getting to the point, but partly also to my frequent interruptions.

He began by explaining that, as joint executors to the will, he and Camilla had spent the previous two days attempting to sort out Edna's belongings, a formidable task and nowhere near completed yet, owing to her tiresome habit of hoarding every scrap of paper which came into her hands, from her birth certificate right down to two- and three-year-old receipts for milk bills. Furthermore, Tilly, who nominally speaking, was Edna's secretary and thus far better equipped for the job had been too immersed in her household duties to help. Her suggestion that Camilla might take over the shopping and housekeeping for a few days had been turned down flat, Camilla nobly insisting that they had all imposed on Tilly for far too long and that it was up to her to manage on her own, for once.

"It was really a joke too, the way she went at it," Ferdy remarked at this point, "I never saw her work so hard at anything before. I think she must have been hoping to turn up a few fivers or something. She was a proper old whirlwind. It's slackened off a bit to-day, but she's nowhere near ready to pack it in."

"And did she turn up any fivers?"

"Couldn't tell you," he replied, after another of his lengthy pauses, then added: "We divided the work up, you see. Separate compartments. It was her idea. She was to go through all Edna's stuff and I'd deal with my father's. Seemed sensible."

"Sensible, you say? I call it daft! Surely there can't be anything left to do with his things? He's been dead for years."

"I know. I expect that was Camilla's idea too, privately, you know. That would be why she gave me the job, wouldn't it? Letting me feel I was being useful, but only where I couldn't make a mess of things. Trouble was, it didn't turn out like that. I haven't told her so, of course."

"Why not?"

"Because she'd be livid and probably feel a bit of an ass, as well; riffling for hours and hours through all those old film magazines and Christmas cards of about fifty years ago; and here's me, with the only really interesting bit sort of more or less falling into my lap."

"How did that happen?"

"Accident, really. All my father's papers were stacked away in that hideous old desk in the library and, like you said, there was nothing to be done. He was a methodical sort of man, not like any of his wives, and any loose ends had been tidied up by Tilly ages ago. The whole lot could have gone on the fire, if my stepmother hadn't been such a miserable hoarder. Does this bore you?"

"No, not at all because I'm all keyed up for the moment when you tell me about finding the secret compartment in one of the drawers."

I couldn't see his face because I had switched off all but the sidelights, but his voice sounded amused:

"No, I didn't. It's just a boring old Victorian desk and I don't suppose it has any secret compartments, but you're getting warm. The middle drawer, the biggest one in the whole outfit, was locked and no key."

" 'Aha!' you said to yourself!"

"I didn't, you know. To be frank with you, Tessa, I was relieved more than anything. 'Well, that lets me out' is what I said to myself."

"But then?"

"But then it hit me that I'd really had it so dead easy, compared to all that load of rubbish Camilla was stuck with, and that I ought at least to jump about a bit, so I asked Tilly if she had any idea where the key was."

"And had she?"

"Not one, but you know Tilly? She's such a conscientious old beaver that she wasn't going to give up till she'd ransacked the entire place from cellar to roof. She finally ran it to earth in one of Edna's bags, the last one she'd been using before she got so ill, and that should have given us the clue."

"To what?"

"Well, I mean, what it pointed to was that she used this drawer all the time and didn't want anyone else to know about the secret things inside it. If you see what I mean?" Ferdy added on a not particularly optimistic note.

"Of course I do, I was only wondering if it had given you a clue as to what these secret things might be?"

"No, and I bet you'd never have guessed either, even though you are so brainy. For instance, did you know that old Edna fancied herself as a writer?"

"No, I must admit that's something I never would have guessed. What sort? Poetry? Fiction?"

"Sort of half and half really. It was written like a novel, none of the 'I this,' 'I the other' business, but you could tell it was really a sort of diary."

"How could you tell?"

"Well, this character, this heroine, I suppose you could say, is called May, goodness knows why but I suppose it was an easy one to spell, and she comes out as very rich and well dressed, full of wisdom and sharp observations, only not too popular because of the witty way she has of putting people down. Even I got the message."

"I see. And is it revealing in other ways too?"

"I don't know about that. Later on there's another character in it called Greta, who's frightfully spoilt and conceited, and there's one called Mattie, who's pretty boring too, so you can see she had a pretty low opinion of us all, if we hadn't known it already. Is that what you meant?"

"No, it wasn't; and listen, Ferdy, fascinated as I am by the fantasy life of E. Mortimer, I must point out that it's getting on for midnight and I still haven't heard one good reason why you should contest the will. If it's because you now have written evidence that she didn't think too highly of you, I should forget it because I doubt if that would cut much ice with the legal profession."

"Oh no, that has nothing to do with it. I got led away by you asking so many questions. The real point is that she was drawing up a new will and I found it, tucked away underneath the diaries. I haven't told anyone about it, except you, and I can't decide whether I ought to or not."

"When you say she was drawing it up, Ferdy, what does that mean exactly? Was it in her own handwriting?"

"No, all typed out in the proper jargon, a straight up lawyers' document. There were one or two blanks, which she'd filled in with a pencil and there were things scribbled in the margin, including some rude remarks. I suppose it was what you'd call a draft."

"Dated?"

"Not the actual day. June of this year."

"In other words, after she'd had at least one attack?"

"Yes, I suppose it must have been."

"Well, come on, Ferdy, let's have it! How was the money carved up?"

"Dead simple. The charities got the same as before, all the rest went to her sister, Alice."

"How about Tilly?"

"Nothing. Makes you think, doesn't it?"

"And nothing for you or Camilla either?"

"Not a penny. We weren't even mentioned."

He faded away into silence again, which this time I welcomed, for I too had much to ponder. Finally I said:

"Well, I see your problem, Ferdy, but it's a moral and not a legal one, isn't it? Legally you're entitled to the money, but if you decide to do the decent thing and hand it over to Alice, that's your business, I should say."

He sighed: "It's not all that simple. I wish it was. Personally, I'm not particularly keen on getting lumbered with all that money. I'd probably grow to love it after a bit and then I'd start worrying that someone was going to come and take it away again. If it was just up to me, I'd as soon get rid of it before it becomes an addiction."

"Then why don't you?"

"Oh, can't you see? There'd be no end of a racket if I did that and everyone would try to talk me out of it. It would drive me dotty and, in the end, I'd find myself telling them about this new will and how Edna had meant to cut me out, just to shut them up, and then we really would be up the creek."

"Because of Camilla, you mean?"

"Right. Tilly too, in a way, but Camilla's the main problem. She's one of those people who really need money more than anything and she was brought up to believe she'd have loads of it. It would be a rotten trick to play on her."

"I don't see why. She'd be under no compulsion to follow your example."

"I know that, but she might feel she was, or that people would expect her to. Even if she didn't do anything about it, can't you see how it would spoil things for her? She'd feel she was behaving less well than someone else, not like a true blue, stainless heroine, and she'd hate that."

It struck me as unlikely that Camilla would have shown as much sensitivity to his feelings, had the boot been on the other foot, or that any little wound to her *amour propre* would not soon be healed by the acquisition of a hundred thousand pounds, but I did not consider it worth while passing these reflections on to Ferdy and I said:

"Well, I hardly see what advice I can give you. It boils down to this: on the one hand, you go against your own grain by accepting the money; on the other, you offend Camilla's susceptibilities by rejecting it. I think you will just have to make up your own mind which is the more important."

"Yes," he agreed, "and isn't it all a damn nuisance?"

"I suppose you could take the money and give it away anonymously?"

"I've thought of that, but I'm afraid it wouldn't work. For one thing, it's going to look funny, me living in a bedsitter in Paddington, and having no car and that, when I'm supposed to be loaded. They'd set the psychiatrists on to me and I wouldn't be able to afford them."

I had learnt enough about human nature to be aware that, whatever appearances may suggest, no one has it easy all the time, but while driving home at last I reflected that this was the first occasion I had met anyone who lay awake at night on account of being lumbered with a hundred thousand pounds. Looking back on it though, what does now strike me as curious is that, for all the elusive, insubstantial quality in Ferdy's personality, making him seem almost one dimensional at times, I never for an instant doubted his sincerity.

CHAPTER FIFTEEN

•

Peter Goodchild, who was not a housemaster, lived with
his wife and two daughters in a flat above the new music
block, which had been built two years earlier with an
endowment fund raised largely through his own efforts.
Thus, as Tara seldom tired of pointing out, they lived over
the shop and a shop, moreover, which had been constructed virtually by their own blood, sweat and tears.

I was admitted to these premises by Leila, the elder
daughter, a sallow-faced girl of about fifteen, with eyes
made of black velvet and long dark hair nipped into two
tightly coiled plaits. She was wearing an embroidered silk
tunic over faded blue jeans, gold thonged sandals and
about fifty-nine assorted bracelets.

Having tossed off the remark that she was engaged in
writing a play based on a little known episode in the life of
Eleanor of Aquitaine, which she judged to be exactly
suited to my prodigious talents, she ushered me into the
sitting room, which also provided a nice example of the
meeting of East and West. There were a lot of highly
coloured cotton rugs, or blankets, hanging on the walls,
along with Rajput miniatures and heavily carved wooden
plaques, but also some impressionist prints and art nou-
veau posters mixed up with them, and an assortment of
musical instruments, including a piano and a sitar. Most of
the seating accommodation consisted of large tooled leather
poufs and a most spectacular oriental touch was provided

by the hostess, seated in the lotus position on a divan
spread with a green and gold sari, bare footed and wearing
an ankle length embroidered silk tunic from the same
stable as Leila's.

Supplying the necessary balance in this respect was
another woman, older and unmistakeably British, sitting
in the most un-lotus position imaginable on the nearest
approach the room contained to an upright armchair. She
was plain and severe looking, with features not unlike her
sister's, but without her florid complexion and petulant
expression, and I had no difficulty in recognising her as
the celebrated water colourist, matron and heiress, Miss
A. Dilloway.

Tara was enchanted with herself for organising this coup,
Alice rather less so. I had fallen into the fatuous error,
partly through hearsay, of assuming that because she was
outwardly a dimmer, less forceful replica of Edna, she
must be equally stupid and vain. Evidently, this was not
the case for, far from echoing Tara's stream of congratulations to all and sundry on bringing the two of us together,
so that I might actually meet the creator of the painting I
had admired so much, Alice responded with an impatient
snort and the observation that she wasn't too keen on
having her leg pulled.

"Who is pulling your leg, my dear Alice? Don't be such
a duffer, please! Our friend here has been saying she is
sick as mud that she cannot buy a ticket for herself in this
raffle. I assure you."

"Then she's a bigger fool than I take her for," Alice
replied tartly. "You know I would never have had the
nerve to exhibit at all, if you hadn't bullied me into it, and
the kindest thing you can say of my paintings is that I'm
only a beginner, didn't take it up until I retired. It gives
me pleasure, but I wouldn't pretend that it's art."

"Well, this is all bosh, my dear. If it were not, why
should I have bought two of your pictures? I am not so
made of money, you know."

"No, you're not, but you have other assets and we both
know that you bought them simply to save me from be-

coming discouraged and giving up my little hobby. Now, be honest, Tara! Isn't that the truth of the matter?"

"No, certainly not, it is a packet of lies and I hope you are not too modest to let Tessa see your pictures and judge for herself?"

"Oh, she can see them if she chooses," Alice said indifferently.

"Good! Then take her to the dining room, pronto, please! While you are there Leila and I will be rustling up some tea."

"I am sure you haven't the least desire to look at them," Alice said when they had gone, thereby placing me in a delicate situation, from which she was kind enough to extricate me in the next breath by adding:

"But I'm afraid you must, because otherwise Tara won't give either of us a minute's peace."

They were two pallid little landscapes, very much in the style of the one I had seen at the exhibition. The first showed a village street of rather eccentric proportions and the second a meadow, with some unidentifiable animals standing about in a listless fashion, as though they had been shot and rather carelessly stuffed. They could, at a pinch, have been horses and I paused rather longer before this one, my mind going back to a certain race meeting six weeks ago.

"You see what I mean?" Alice asked in her caustic way.

"It's more than I could do," I replied truthfully and then, convinced by this time that her diffidence was not assumed, I added:

"And, anyway, I don't see it matters how bad they are, so long as doing them gives you pleasure."

"I agree with you, it shouldn't really matter at all, but the trouble with Tara is that all her geese are swans and have to behave like swans, for their own good. She's such a dear, but it does embarrass me when she will foist my wretched daubs on other people."

So far, Alice had scarcely uttered a word that bore out her reputation, so I set her another test:

"I was so sorry to hear about Mrs. Mortimer."

"Were you?" she replied, keeping the record intact. "Why was that?"

"Well . . . I can't pretend to have been very fond of her, or anything, but I had known her for an awfully long time; ever since Camilla and I were twelve years old, in fact," then realising that this was somewhat inadequate grounds for professing grief, I went on:

"Also I was sitting with her for a short while only the day before she died and it was rather distressing."

"Yes, it must have been."

"I don't mean only because she was so ill. As a matter of fact, there'd been a slight improvement at that point and everyone thought she had a fair chance of recovering."

"Then what was distressing about it?"

"Well, you see, she had one of her lucid periods while I was with her and she was trying so hard to tell me something urgent, I could sense that she was; something she was frightened about, or that was the impression I got, but she couldn't speak and when she tried to write some words on a pad she was so weak that it was impossible to decipher them. What makes me sad is that she should have died with that awful secret locked up inside her, and nobody was ever able to find out what it was and give her comfort."

"You seem to know a good deal more about my sister's last hours than I do," Alice remarked stiffly.

"Well, as I say, no one realised those would be her last hours. They thought she was improving. It was pure chance that I happened to be there at the time."

"Excuse me, but I don't think chance had much to do with it. I think you were called in, weren't you? Requested to go? And by Miss Prettyman, no doubt?"

After a slight hesitation, due mainly to the fact that this was the first time for years that I had heard Tilly referred to by that name, I said:

"No, the suggestion came from Camilla, actually."

"It amounts to the same thing. Camilla was the mouthpiece. She very often is, but that's not important. The fact remains that you were called in, whereas I was kept out; if not by force, as near as makes no matter."

"Oh, surely not?"

"Oh yes, indeed! That is the truth of the matter, Miss Crichton, although I wouldn't expect you to believe me. I daresay you have been brainwashed, along with everyone else."

"Brainwashed? By Til . . . Miss Prettyman?"

"Yes, my dear, by Miss Prettyman."

"But what on earth for? I mean, why should she bother to do that?"

Alice turned away and walked over to the window, which overlooked some playing fields and beyond them, a quiet, willow shaded stretch of the river. There was something contemplative in her attitude, which gave me the sinking feeling that she was studying the scene with a view to painting it at some future time, but when she spoke again it was on a brisk, faintly sardonic note:

"You remind me of one of my patients, Eileen somebody or other she was called. Nice quiet girl, no trouble to anyone, except that she used to waste the nurses' time. She had this trick, gift you might prefer to call it, of getting them to talk about themselves and there they'd be perched on her bed, pouring it all out, and the rest of the ward in an uproar, for all they cared. She was only in for a week or two, for which I was thankful, but a few years later I found myself standing next to her in a theatre queue. I wouldn't have recognised her, but she remembered me at once and she told me more about my staff nurse than I'd learnt in five years daily contact."

I did not consider that any comment was expected of me, so made none and Alice continued:

"It may surprise you to learn that Edna and I were the most devoted of sisters until about ten years ago?"

"Were you? What broke it up?"

"She was a year or two older than me, but I was acknowledged to be the clever one of the family and Edna never resented that. After all, she was the pretty one, and she was pretty too, in those days. Even though I was in a lower form at school, she used to get me to help her with her homework and when we grew up it had become second nature to her to ask my advice on every subject under the sun, even her boy friends. I didn't have many of them, didn't want them either, and I think she valued my detachment, as well as respecting my opinions. There was never any jealousy on either side."

Alice paused here, in the manner of one reviewing the past and considering whether her present assessment of it was correct, and I repeated my question:

"Why did things change? Was it because of her marriage?"

"Not her first marriage, no. Curiously enough, things went on just the same after that. Jack, that was her first husband, and I hit it off very well and he didn't seem to mind at all that she wanted to include me in so many of their activities. We even used to go on holiday together. They didn't have any children, of course. That might have made a difference, but then again it might not. I think Jack and I both knew, dearly though we loved her, that Edna could be impatient and impetuous at times and apt to become self-pitying over the most trifling grievances. I think she might have made a poor job of bringing up children, if she'd been left to it on her own. That we shall never know, but still, as I say, our threesome lasted all through her first marriage and when Jack died I was the only one she could bear to have near her. She was very sorry for herself then, couldn't believe that God could be so cruel, and as a result she became more dependent on me than ever. It got to the point where her demands were beginning to interfere with my work and, not only that, I couldn't help seeing that I was doing her more harm than good by constantly propping her up, until she was incapable of standing on her own feet. It seems funny, looking back on it and remembering what a job I had persuading her to go on that cruise. I almost had to carry her on board; and three weeks later, when she came home, she hardly bothered to let me know."

"Having met husband number two under the Grecian stars?"

Alice smiled: "That about sums it up. She was quite girlish and romantic again. I doubt if Mr. Mortimer saw things in exactly the same light, but then I'm told that both his former wives had been vain, frivolous creatures,

so perhaps he wasn't disappointed in her. Can't have
been, since he left her every penny he had. All the same,
she was never his wife in the true sense. It was Miss
Prettyman who ran the show, just as she always had. And,
not content with that, she had to oust me as well."

"Meaning that your sister transferred her loyalty?"

"Loyalty, affection, dependence, the lot; and all in a
matter of months. I wouldn't have minded, at any rate not
so badly, if it had been for Edna's good, but of course it
wasn't. Instead of putting a curb on her weaknesses, Miss
Prettyman did her utmost to foster them. She soft soaped
her from morning till night, indulged her in every selfish
whim that came into her head and never allowed her to do
a hand's turn. And, of course, when Mr. Mortimer died it
was all up. Miss Prettyman had thoroughly succeeded in
setting Edna against me by then, so she had it all her own
way. It was the death of her too, in my opinion."

"Oh, surely that's exaggerating a bit, Miss Dilloway?
I can understand your resentment, but after all she
was seriously overweight and, with high blood pressure,
and . . ."

"Yes, and why was that, I'd like to know? Lolling about
all day, never moving a yard on her own two feet, eating
little snacks between meals and drinking little nips of
champagne whenever she felt depressed or out of sorts.
Who wouldn't be overweight? Who wouldn't have high
blood pressure?"

Leila appeared in the doorway:

"Mummie's going to have high blood pressure if you
don't both come and drink your tea," she informed us.
"She says it's getting stewed to old rags. I don't know
where she picks up these colourful expressions," she added,
giving my arm a squeeze as she propelled me from the
room. "I sometimes suspect her of sneaking down to the
Lower School library for an orgy of Dornford Yates."

CHAPTER SIXTEEN

•

Hearts and hopes were high in the old Methodist Chapel that night, for news had reached us that Mr. Winter was taking up his option to bring the play into London, as soon as a suitable theatre became available, and plans were already in hand for the provincial tour.

None of this had been beyond our expectations, for we had played to packed chapels ever since opening and all seats for the last three performances had been sold a week in advance. There could be no doubt either that the audiences had enjoyed themselves, but, sadly, even this combination provided no guarantee of security in the chancy world we inhabited and it was a relief to know that for the next few months, at least, we should be sailing through calm waters.

One small cold draught continued to whistle round some of the dressing rooms, in so far as it was rumoured that there were to be some minor cast changes, but Toby informed me in confidence that he believed that nepotism was still a force in the theatre and that, whatever my shortcomings, I need have no fear that the axe would fall on me.

"Well, thanks awfully," I said, "I'm most appreciative. I imagine that's the kind of thing Shakespeare used to say to Burbage. And talking of these historical figures, Toby, which you are rather more up in than me, do you consider it at all probable that most of the people Richelieu was

surrounded by in his lifetime regarded him as a sweet old
gentleman, devoted to children and dogs?"

"No."

"You don't envisage any possibility that all the *eminence
grise* stuff came later? Put about after his death by jealous
rivals, wishing to discredit him for posterity?"

"No."

"Are you really applying yourself to these questions,
Toby?"

"No."

"I thought not, and yet it is a fact that neither people
nor events are always what they seem."

"Yes."

"Of necessity, one sees them mostly from a single point
of view, and not always a first hand one at that. Quite
often one takes things about them on trust and, where
required to, trims one's personal experience to fit the
general picture."

"It is the only thing one can do, I suppose."

"Without stopping to ask oneself if personal experience
really matches up with pre-conceived notions."

"Very true! Are we speaking in specific terms, by the
way, or just wandering down some little path into abstract-
ville?"

"I am speaking specifically of two people."

"That's taking on rather a lot, isn't it, at this hour of the
morning?"

"It can't be helped. They go together like a horse and
carriage and you can't have one without the other. The
question is this: is one right and the other wrong, or are
they both half right and half wrong?"

"I find it terribly difficult to judge," he admitted, "from
the evidence so far before me. It might help, I don't say it
would, but it might help if I knew who we were talking
about."

"A saint and a villain and I don't know which is which."

Toby sighed: "I hate riddles. I think I'll go for a walk."

"No, stay for just five more minutes. I know I'm not
making sense, but it's only because all my pre-conceived
ideas have suddenly been turned upside down and I haven't

got used to it yet. Ever since I first came to stay here, I've had two well known, self-evident truths thrust under my nose. One was that Tilly was an angel from heaven, unselfish, uncomplaining and steady as a rock. . . ."

"And the other?"

"That Alice was her exact opposite. A disappointed, disagreeable, quarrelsome old gorgon, who went about stirring up trouble in every quarter."

"And who is now daring to question these well-known, self-evident truths?"

"Well, Tara Goodchild for one, I suspect, if we were to ask her. So far as I know, she's scarcely aware of Tilly's existence, except as a sort of appendage to Edna, and probably tarred with her brush. Edna, as we all know, was that worst of philistines, the rich woman who wouldn't contribute a penny for the arts. On the other hand, she obviously regards Alice, who until recently has never had a penny to contribute towards anything, with high favour."

'I have heard it said that one swallow doesn't make an Indian summer."

"So have I, but I take my own judgement into account as well."

"Yes, I suppose one would be bound to."

"I was prepared for the worst with Alice, but in fact she was perfectly friendly and amiable. Streets ahead of Edna in every way. I agree that wouldn't be hard, but it was different from anything I had expected."

"Led by Tilly to expect?"

"Yes, and by Camilla and Vi and Marge and a whole lot more. In other words, everyone who belongs in the Tilly league, but doesn't know Alice particularly well. And Alice made one extremely acute remark. She said that although a particular suggestion might have come from Camilla it was more likely to have been inspired by Tilly. Now, we all know how clever Tilly is in that way, but I'd taken it for granted that she used the talent constructively, to build people up, in fact. It had never occurred to me before that there might also be a destructive element in it. You see where all this is leading, of course?"

"Oh, of course," he replied, more from the desire to silence me, I daresay, than from conviction.

"It is leading straight back to Richelieu," I said, dashing these forlorn hopes.

"Oh, God!"

"Because if you are correct in maintaining that no one could wield a dark and evil power during their lifetime and simultaneously acquire a reputation for being harmless and kind, then, despite appearances, Alice must be a jealous vindictive woman, who spends her time manufacturing grievances which have no basis, in which case we have nothing to worry about."

"I am not in the least worried."

"Maybe not, but I am. I've always believed that though Tilly may be a fond and foolish old woman in some ways, she hadn't a deceitful or unkind thought in her head. I'd hate to have to change my mind about that, but now along comes Alice, who, conversely, doesn't appear to be nearly so black as she's been painted, with the news that Tilly is a scheming harpy, pushing Edna into her grave and cutting her off from the one person who truly had her welfare at heart. When you add the fact that Tilly had a slap up motive, well, it makes you think, doesn't it?"

"If you're referring to Edna's new will, I don't see that it gave her any better motive than Ferdy or Camilla. They both stood to lose just as much or more by it."

"We all know that now, but we didn't when Edna was alive. The only one who probably knew about both wills was Tilly. The key to the drawer where it was kept turns up in one of Edna's bags, oh what a surprise! But I bet you fifty thousand pounds that Tilly could have laid her hands on it any time she wanted to."

"And jolly good luck to her, if she did! I consider Edna behaved disgracefully in cutting her out. And, incidentally, since Tilly had become so indispensable to her, why was she to be cut out? Have you found the answer to that one yet?"

"No, but there are various possibilities, including the one that Alice's verdict was right and Edna had finally begun to see this for herself, without any prompting, or that Alice had succeeded in getting the message across. So that still leaves the question open as to which of those two was the *eminence grise* and which the *blanche*. One thing we do know is that if anyone was impersonating Edna, out of malice or for a more sinister purpose, it's unlikely to have been Alice. Her best bet was obviously to keep her sister in good fettle until the new will had been made legal."

"No, you're quite wrong there," Toby said, getting up and moving towards the door. "I'm going for my walk now. The five minutes were up hours ago."

"All the same, you might at least tell me before you go why I'm quite wrong there."

"In the first place, there's no guarantee that Alice knew anything about a new will, but was simply anxious to get her hands on her original share before she was too old to enjoy it. Secondly, if she did know, she could have been under the impression that it had already been signed, in which case it would have been imperative to work fast, before Edna could change her mind yet again and start revoking that one."

"Which brings us back to where we started?"

"It's too bad, I agree, but something tells me you won't easily persuade either of those two to open up their hearts to you on this subject, and unfortunately it is now too late for Edna to do so."

"And that's where you're quite wrong there," I said with a faint lilt of triumph, which soared a note or two higher when I saw that he was no longer in quite such a hurry to leave.

"What can you mean, Tessa?"

"I don't exactly know how it is to be done," I admitted, "but I do know that the possibility exists. Off you go for your walk now and perhaps I'll have hit on the answer by the time you get back."

CHAPTER SEVENTEEN

•

An hour or two later, at noon to be precise, I entered the premises of Ladye Fayre, which is the name of Storhampton's grandest hairdressing salon, for my regular daily comb-out.

I do not normally go to such lengths to keep my appearance up to the mark, but there was a scene, supposedly of a public performance of our play within a play, where, with off stage passions running high and mutiny breaking out all over, the actor who played my adoring husband in the interior play, if I may so describe it, and my implacable enemy in the exterior one, was required to lose his temper with me, in wholly unscripted fashion. This led to his walking off at the end of the scene and slamming the door behind him, a contingency which had not been allowed for by the amateur set constructors and stage management, with the result that a chunk of scenery fell down, part of it on my head.

I had complained about this several times, but the director had pointed out that as the joke always went down like a high explosive bomb, giving rise, to quote a well known source, to such hilarity and mirth, it would be a crime to drop it and that I could always overcome the personal inconvenience by wearing a wig. However, I was equally opposed to that suggestion and hence my daily appointment with Ladye Fayre.

On this occasion there was a customer occupying the

chair next to mine, whose vaguely familiar features beneath the heavy rollers turned out on closer inspection to be those of Helena Plowman. For some strange reason, my initial reaction was to assume that she had been planted there in answer to some unspoken prayer and while Mr. Percy was teasing away at my hair a small elusive memory was also doing some teasing in the regions just below it. However, before I had succeeded in nailing it down Helena had been led away and was by then incarcerated and incommunicado, under the dryer.

At this point, I tried to dismiss the memory as of no special consequence, but it responded by taking a firmer grip on me than ever and all the time I was removing the nylon overall, bringing out money for the bill and agreeing with Mrs. Percy that it did look as though we were in for another scorcher and who'd want to go to Spain in a summer like this, I was also hearing Robin's voice, when in one of our discussions about Edna he had reminded me that, with only one reservation, involving a conspiracy, anyone who could not have impersonated her doppelganger on even a single appearance must be absolved from all the others too. I finally allowed it to rule me and left a note for Helena at the reception desk, inviting her to join me for a Special Lunch at the Jolly Angler as soon as she could get away.

"My dear, this is very civil of you," she said, sitting down fifteen minutes later at the table I had procured in the window.

She was wearing the identical pleated shirtwaister as on the previous occasion, except that this one was cream instead of toffee-coloured and she looked so pristine and immaculate that if I had not known better I should have suspected her of having been home to change in the interval.

"Not at all," I replied. "I hate lunching alone and, besides, I owe you one."

Needless to say, neither of these arguments had influenced me in the slightest; nor had the invitation been extended in order to gain a first hand report on the ups and downs, rewards and losses, heartbreaks etcetera of the Festival, although I encouraged her to unburden herself on these topics, believing that my objective would be more easily achieved after a little preliminary softening up.

Perhaps I overdid it, because half way through the flabby fish she said:

"Well now, Tessa, you're very patient, but I can't seriously believe that you're interested in all these facts and figures, which make up my life at the moment. Tell me about yourself. How's everything going?"

"Pretty fair, thank you. Mustn't grumble. Your hair's looking a treat, by the way."

"Oh, thank you," she said in a rather flustered way, instinctively raising a hand to pat or twiddle, then recollecting herself and dropping it like a hot coal. "I think they do it quite well. Not exactly Dover Street standards, naturally, but they do take trouble and I've trained them not to keep me waiting, which is a great asset."

"Do you always go there?"

"Oh yes, always," she replied without hesitation. "It's so convenient, for one thing. Besides, there isn't another place in Storhampton where one could go, as far as I know. Is there?"

"No, but Tilly was raving about somewhere in Stourbury and, just to prove how marvellous and utterly superior it was, she told me that you patronised it."

Helena opened her mouth, then leant back in her chair and stared at me in a very unnerving way. I could not decide whether her look expressed annoyance, incredulity or even some quite different emotion because, as always when she was concentrating, the squint appeared and made her expression as inscrutable as a Buddhist monk's.

"In fact," I galloped on before she had a chance to shut me up, "it was having just met you there which set her off on it. I remember so well because I had been to Stourbury races with Vi and Marge and we had to collect Tilly at a bus stop. There was a bit of panic on because it was the afternoon Mrs. Mortimer was taken ill, only none of us knew it at the time, only that she was missing. Tilly was saying that she'd been to the hairdressers and met you there, and what a coincidence and so on and so forth. You know how she rattles on?"

Helena had been picking away with a finger-nail at a tiny hole in the tablecloth, while I rattled on myself, and now laughed in a very unamused way:

"I do indeed! She's a great talker, but unfortunately for me no one could ever accuse her of straying from the truth. Be sure your sins will find you out, Tessa!"

"Oh, what a pity!"

"The fact is," Helena said, looking at me squarely at last, "I'm going a bit grey here and there and I don't terribly like it to be known. Something to do with hating to grow old, I suppose. So I have it tinted three or four times a year. My one small, secret vanity, you might say."

"But why secret?" I asked, completely non-plussed.

"Oh well, you know what a hotbed of gossip this place is? If I had it done locally, no one would allow me a single natural hair on my head. It would be all over the town in no time that I was completely grey and a thorough old fake. It was unlucky for me that Tilly happened to have an appointment at the same time as mine. She hasn't a spiteful thought in her head, but, as you say, she is rather a chatterbox. I suppose I could have warned her not to give me away, but that might have sounded as though there were something to be ashamed of, which I don't consider there is. I mean, look how I've come clean with you, Tessa! And, incidentally, I know I can trust you not to pass it on?"

At one moment during this rather self-contradictory confession, I began to experience the sensation of a thunderous great wave gathering force somewhere just behind me and, by the time she had finished speaking, I could have sworn it had actually swept over me, knocking me off my feet and leaving me washed up and gasping on the beach.

Evidently noticing this, Helena said sharply: "Well, there's no need to gape at me like a dying fish, Tessa! I'm not the only woman in the world to have her hair tinted, you know."

"Of course not," I mumbled. "I wasn't staring because

of that. To tell you the truth, I was wondering why it
should bother you so much? I change my own to any
colour of the rainbow, any time I feel like it. What does it
matter?"

"It matters quite a lot at my age, as you'll find out one
of these days. And now, if you'll forgive me, I'll dispense
with coffee and get back to my desk. The Festival may be
nearly over for some, but there's still a mass of clearing
up to do behind the scenes."

I was grateful to her for cutting this rather awkward
scene short, leaving me to cogitate in peace while I drank
my coffee and waited for the bill, for as for having a mass
of clearing up to do, she wasn't the only one.

The first piece of debris to find its way into the mental
waste-paper basket was the one which had Tilly's name on
it. Since she had now been provided by an unbiassed
witness with an unassailable alibi for the first of the ghostly
appearances, there was, according to Robin's dictum, only
the most outlandish and implausible reason for keeping it
around to clutter up the issue. No matter how conscien-
tiously I tried to find a way round it, there was simply no
possibility of her having spent a full hour, which was the
minimum she would have required, at a hairdressers in
the centre of the town, if the afternoon's programme had
also included her presence in the centre of the race course
between three and four p.m.

Her departure was quickly followed by Ferdy's. There
was no clear cut evidence to dictate his dismissal, but the
little I had seen of him during the past few weeks had
almost convinced me that he possessed neither the temperament nor guile, far less the will to form and carry out
such a plan. Furthermore, if he had gone to the trouble of
dressing up and passing himself off as an elderly woman,
he would not then have undone all the bad work by
maintaining, truthfully or otherwise, on a later occasion
that he had seen the so-called phantom too and that there
was nothing supernatural about it. Finally, if the first two
circumstances had not been present, it would still have
been necessary to find him a plausible incentive, since he

had proved himself to be immune to the financial one. Had it been otherwise, he had only to have kept quiet about the new will, have destroyed it and thereafter denied all knowledge of its existence.

Bernard and Camilla still hovered on the fringes, since, separately and together, they had had the best of opportunities throughout, though I doubted whether either possessed the daring for such an enterprise. More to the point, Camilla's frenzied hunt through her grandmother's papers was ample proof, so far as I was concerned, that she did know of the existence of the new will, which would have made her penniless, but certainly did not know that it was unsigned and invalid. It followed almost inevitably that her hopes would have been centred on keeping Edna alive until such time as she had contrived to work herself back into favour again.

It was a sad ruin of my beautiful theory to be left with, after all the trouble that had gone into constructing it and I still could not bring myself to discard it utterly, for I was stuck with the nagging conviction that no one so prosaic and dull as Edna could have genuinely suffered from or possessed the imagination to invent those strange hallucinations, plus the fact that so many people stood to gain so much by her death. These factors, combined perhaps with the knowledge that an anti-climactic period was about to set in, with the Festival nearly over and the tour not ready to begin, made me resolve to have one last stab at getting to the truth before throwing in the sponge. There was, in addition, the memory of that tidal wave which had so unexpectedly engulfed me while Helena was talking and of the revelation it had seemed to leave behind when it receded; but this dictated an entirely new approach to the problem, and one which required careful thought and planning.

CHAPTER EIGHTEEN

•

1

My proud announcement that I hoped to hit on a means to acquaint myself with the needs of a dead woman's heart before Toby returned from his walk had not been all hot air, but I was beginning to regret that he had not set out to tramp to San Francisco and back.

Various methods had come to mind, including the good old stand-by of wanting to build up the characterisation of a part I was preparing for, which had served me on various occasions in the past to obtain information which was not strictly my business, but in the end I discarded them all. Since the only hand which could turn this particular key for me was Ferdy's, I eventually came to the conclusion that the best hope of getting his co-operation lay in following his own example and approaching the subject by the most direct route available.

I therefore used the interval between performances to go across to the Jolly Angler, where he was often to be found at that hour of the evening, totting up the gains and losses from the current day's racing results and planning future strategy.

This turned out exactly as I had hoped and when I had bought myself a drink, to save all the rigmarole of his borrowing the money to buy one for me, I asked him if he had any hot tips for the following day.

"There's a horse called Bitter Aloes at Doncaster, which I rather fancy," he replied.

"Oh, me too! If you're backing it, put an extra pound on, will you?" I said, not forgetting to hand over the stake.

"Okay, but what's so special for you about Bitter Aloes?"

"Only that he did me a big favour about six weeks ago at Stourbury."

Ferdy was now regarding me with awe, if not actual reverence.

"Twenty-five to one, or was it thirty? You don't mean to say you backed him, Tessa?"

"That's right. I'll tell you another who did too, and that was your stepmother."

"Well, bully for her! Was that on your advice?"

"No, as a matter of fact I understood her to say that the tip came from you."

He shook his head sadly and no one had ever looked less embarrassed or guilty:

"Only wish it had. I went for the favourite in that race, I remember, and it wasn't even placed. What do you want to do this time, win or each way? I'm afraid you won't get half that price now."

It had been a pure formality really, and nothing to be disappointed about in his reaction, which had been very much what I had expected. It was simply one more item swept out of the way in the clearing up process.

On the credit side, however, it made as good a lever as I was likely to find for introducing the main topic and when he had finished noting down my instructions in his niggly, immature hand, and anticipated a favourable outcome to them by spending my pound on another round of drinks, I said in what I hoped were musing tones:

"It's funny about Edna, you know. I'm beginning to think there was a good deal more to her than met the eye."

"Oh yes?"

"Take this business of Bitter Aloes; why should she have bothered to conceal her source of information? The race was already over, so how could it have mattered? And then there's that extraordinary diary you told me she kept, and the fact that she was secretly drawing up this new will, cutting out all the people who'd been closest to her and had the most right to inherit your father's money. By the way, Ferdy, have you decided yet what you're going to do about that?"

"No, but they're saying now that it'll be months before they work out the probate and all that, so I don't have to move in a hurry. They offered me an advance, if I wanted it, but I don't. I'd rather not commit myself, you see. Sort of stalling for time, really."

"Your time will run out eventually."

"I know, but I'm keeping my fingers crossed that before it does something will turn up to make the decision for me; let me off the hook, if you know what I mean?"

"You haven't discussed it with anyone else?"

"No, only you. Why?"

"I was thinking of a girl friend, or someone like that."

"There is a girl, as a matter of fact," he said, staring moodily into his beer. "She's in London. We get on quite well, but she's always trying to smarten me up and talk me into doing the kind of things I don't really know how to do properly, and I have a nasty feeling I know what her answer to this one would be. It could end with my losing her as well."

And, personally, I had a nasty feeling he was likely to do so in any case, the way he was drifting through life, but this was one problem which did not concern me and I said:

"I've thought of one way I might be able to help you."

"Gosh, have you really, Tessa? That's terrific! I always said you were a genius!"

"Don't get carried away because I only said 'might'. There's no guarantee that it will work out."

"Still, anything's worth a try. What was your idea?"

"Well, going back to that peculiar sort of diary you found in the locked drawer, remember?"

"Yes," he said hesitantly, looking, as I had feared, both puzzled and disappointed.

"How much of it did you actually read?"

"Oh, hardly any, as a matter of fact."

"I thought not," I said, endeavouring to hide my relief.

"Well, it was the most awful drivel, you know. Sad, in a way too. I didn't fancy ploughing through much of it."

"Would you allow me to?"

"Plough through it yourself? Whatever for?"

"Not necessarily all of it, that would depend. I'd be looking for something in particular, you see, which may or may not be there. It would probably mean bending the rules a little because, strictly speaking, I suppose Camilla ought to be consulted, but we can't very well ask her permission without explaining why and, as I understand it, secrecy is your watchword?"

"Well, yes, that's right, but I only didn't want her to find out about this new will until I've decided what action to take. I can't see any harm in telling her about the silly old diary."

"But don't you understand, Ferdy, it's more than likely that the two things are connected? That's the whole point. I don't know about you, but personally I find it hard to believe that even someone as prickly and impulsive as your stepmother would turn people from paupers to plutocrats and back again, with a wave of her wand, just because they'd forgotten to fill her hot water bottle or something. She must have had a sound motive for wanting to change her will, and whatever it was may be tucked somewhere in that diary."

"I daresay you're right," Ferdy agreed. "Well, yes, I suppose you have to be, and it was fearfully bright of you to think of it; but, honestly, Tessa, is it going to make all that difference to know why she did it? I mean, however dotty her reasons may seem to us, they must have been important to her, otherwise she wouldn't have acted on them, so I can't see how knowing would help very much."

This was a tricky one and I answered it in a grave and heavy tone, hoping to lend substance to a somewhat flimsy argument:

"I honestly believe it could make all the difference. For instance, supposing it should turn out that she wasn't seriously intending to disinherit you and Camilla, after all?

In other words, that this was just one more stick to beat you with, and Tilly too, for that matter?"

"I thought of that," he admitted. "It was the kind of trick she often went in for when she thought she wasn't getting her share of attention, but I think if this had been one of those she would just have told us about it, don't you? My point is, Tessa, I don't believe she'd have gone to the trouble and expense of getting it drawn up by lawyers unless it was for real."

"Yes, she would," I said firmly. "You've just admitted it was the kind of game she enjoyed playing and she could have realised that she'd cried Wolf once too often. On the other hand, if she'd waved an official looking document under your noses and read bits of it aloud to you, none of you would have guessed that she hadn't signed it and had no intention of doing so, and you'd all have worked twice as hard at getting back into favour. At least, you probably wouldn't, but the others might have and, with her low view of human nature, that's certainly the result she'd have been expecting."

"You could be right, I suppose, but where does all this get us? I've rather lost track."

"Well, don't you see, Ferdy, that if I can prove this theory, to the point where you and I are satisfied that she meant the old will to stand and the other was just a phoney, then you're in the clear? You can tear it up and forget about it; you can refuse the money, or accept it and give the whole lot away, or anything you damn well please. It will be up to you entirely and the best part of all will be that Camilla can take her whack with a clear conscience and never have to feel that she was cheating."

I managed to infuse quite an impassioned note into the last bit and, if I'd had any conscience at all, it must have been wrung when Ferdy not only beamed his approval of my clever scheme, but actually thanked me most sincerely for offering to wade through Edna's diary.

2

It looked like Christmas Day at the Chapel when I returned there on Wednesday evening, after this interlude. Our play, having been chosen to open the Festival of Drama, was necessarily the first to close and this was to be our final public performance. Nevertheless, I felt quite overwhelmed by the many unexpected tributes.

There was quite a pile of fan letters, even including a few whose writers did not ask for signed, six by four photographs; also a slender white box, with an elegant and even slenderer ballpoint inside it, which could have been gold for all I knew. It had my initials engraved on it and had come from the generous hand of Mr. David Winter.

As well as this, there were eight magnificent Fragrant Clouds, wrapped in pretty pink *Financial Times*, from Toby's garden, which would have been inexpressibly touching, were it not for the fact that immediately after the show they were destined to be taken straight back to their starting point; and finally there was a letter addressed in an unfamiliar hand, but starting off: "My dear Eileen".

It continued as follows:

"I hope you won't feel this is taking an advantage of your kindness in listening to me so patiently the other afternoon, but I have run into a spot of bother, which you may be able to help with. I have an old school friend staying with me at present, who is most anxious to see the play (she is a particular fan of yours!) and I had promised to get seats for this evening. Unfortunately, as you can understand, my sister's death put all thoughts of this kind out of my head and I had forgotten every word about it until my friend arrived yesterday and reminded me of it almost before she had her coat off. Now, alas, I find I am too late and that all the tickets have been sold (Congratulations!). The young lady at the box office has advised us to try again an hour before the performance, just in case any have been returned, but she does not hold out much hope of this and I am making so bold as to ask if you have any 'pull', which would save the day for us? We don't mind at all where we sit—two singles, if necessary—and I need hardly say that we should insist on paying!"

Several words in this text had been underlined, including the last three, but as it happened neither her willingness to pay the price of each ticket thirty times over, nor cedarwood, sandalwood and sweet white wine from Nineveh would have availed her anything, and I knew for a fact that the house seats had already been claimed as well.

However, I had no wish to jeopardise the cordial relationship between myself and Alice and, furthermore, I could see some positive advantage in meeting the old school friend, so immediately dashed off a note, which I left with the young lady in the box office.

Having expressed regret for my inability to overcome her sad predicament, I added that, as she was no doubt already aware, we were giving a special free matinee the following morning for some of the chronically handicapped inmates of the local hospital (having been coerced into this, although I did not mention it, by her friend, Tara) and, provided she had no objection to seeing the play under these conditions, I would do my best to wangle a couple of tickets.

I then added a postscript, though not an afterthought, saying that in the event of her taking up this offer, I hoped she would bring her friend round to see me after the show and tell me what they had thought of it.

CHAPTER NINETEEN

•

"Well, I see you've waded through Vols. One to Three,"
Toby said, as I closed another of the four fat exercise
books which Ferdy had delivered that morning. "Any luck
yet?"

"Nothing to the point, although one or two interesting
facts have emerged. The bulk of it is absolute self-dramatising
drivel, though; Ferdy was quite right there."

"Had you expected to unearth another Fanny Burney?"

"No, but I hadn't bargained for its being quite so childish, or so confusing. It's only dated by the day of the
week, for a start and there seem to be large gaps when the
Muse deserted her, only it's impossible to be sure how
large they are. At one minute this so-called niece, who is a
droopy, selfish girl and obviously meant for Camilla, but
referred to as Greta, is a schoolgirl and a page or two later
she's going to be married."

"Who to? I mean, what name does he go under?"

"George. Quite suitable, in a way, I suppose; steady,
unimaginative and rather dull. On the other hand, she
doesn't bother to change all the names, or at any rate
hardly at all. Mattie, for instance, is only another variation
on Matilda, i.e. Tilly; and her lawyer is called Bertie,
which is sometimes used as a shortening of Robert. Her
husband is called Benny, which incidentally strikes me as
a supremely unsuitable name for that pompous old graven

111

image, but presumably it was how she addressed him in private."

"And is that one of the interesting facts that has so far emerged?"

"No, although there is a connection because there are several references to a mysterious woman called Fay, who appears to have designs on Benny, believe it or not. And May and Fay, you notice? So if Fay's a pseudonym too, it was rather a curious choice."

"Perhaps invention ran out; or perhaps they're the good and wicked fairies? What sort of designs does Wicked have?"

"Oh, the usual. From Good's description, it practically amounts to alienation of affections. She's always trying to insinuate herself into their lives, to cut May out and try and make her look a fool. Would probably have succeeded, too, as far as I can gather, if May hadn't been so sweet and beautiful, ha ha, that Benny was absolutely bonkers about her. But don't you agree that it's curious, Toby? Did you ever hear of any scandal of that sort in connection with old Benjamin?"

"Never. Upright as a tombstone. I mean, he went after lots of women, but he always married them."

"That's what I thought. And yet one can hardly conceive that Edna would have made it up. What would be the point, since it was never intended to be read by anyone but herself?"

"God knows. What became of Fay eventually? Did Edna see her off?"

"She simply faded out when poor old Benny died. She would have, of course, and soon after that a woman called Bella becomes the villain of the piece. Not for the same reason, naturally; this one is just bossy and dowdy and terribly interfering. And this is where the second interesting fact emerges. I do wish dear old May had been a bit more precise about dates, but as far as I can make out the incident she describes must have occurred at least six months ago because it comes before the part where Greta and George announce their engagement."

"Is the date so important?"

"Yes, very, because if I'm right, it means that it also occurred at least six months before her first recorded vision of the doppelganger."

"You imply that there had been an earlier, unrecorded one?"

"Sounds like it; at the V. and A., of all places!"

"Now, that's what I do call an interesting fact. Are you quite sure this is a real diary and not just straight fiction?"

"It seems there was some special exhibition on at the time. Naturally, she doesn't mention what it was; only terrible moans about their having to queue for hours to get in."

"They?"

"Yes, she was taken there by dowdy old Bella, who seems to have had artistic pretensions, to add to all her other unattractive qualities."

"And did Bella see the double too?"

"That part is not very explicit. Perhaps, if I were to read it out to you, it might convey something?"

Toby nodded gloomily and I picked up Vol. Three, which fell open at the page I had marked, and then set the scene for him, before beginning to read:

"You must now picture her as being flattened with fatigue after all that standing around in the street and she and Bella are taking a short rest on a couch in one of the anterooms to the exhibition. The queue, in fact, is now filing past them. Got that? Right, so here it comes!

" 'Of a sudden', yes, I'm afraid she's keen on expressions like that, 'Of a sudden, May found herself staring as though mesmerised by one face in this sea of faces who were pushing past her. Could it be true?' "

"I should hardly think so," Toby muttered.

"Never mind! Her style may be a little more on the purple side than your own, but you will get used to it. I'll continue:

" 'Could it be true? she asked herself with a dreadful tremor of fear, or did she merely imagine that the woman she was gazing at was in truth herself? Unable to speak or voice her fears, she instinctively placed one slender, trembling hand on her companion's arm, pointing shakily

*with the other. What's the matter? Bella cried in alarm.
Look . . . look over there . . . May begged, summoning
the last ounce of her strength. That . . . woman . . . is
she . . . Me? Exhausted and confused, she fell forward in
a dead faint and remembered nothing more for several
minutes.*

"And that's a pity, isn't it, Toby? It's those several
minutes which are crucial. If only she had not collapsed in
a dead faint, we might now have the categorical answer as
to whether these apparitions were actual or imaginary; or
whether someone was already following her around in
order to play tricks on her. Still, we now have part of the
answer, which is something to be going on with."

"Which part?"

"We know that she didn't invent them, to make herself
interesting or pathetic, or as a form of emotional black-
mail, as some people have suggested. Hallucinations or
not, they were obviously real and terrifying to her, so that
in a sense I feel vindicated."

"I can see you would; and slightly smug as well, but it
sounds as though you are no nearer to finding out whether
someone was deliberately impersonating her, still less who
that could have been."

"No, but I suppose I needn't give up just yet. There is
still one door left open, you know. I could find out whether
Bella is a real name, or another pseudonym; and, if so,
what her real name is and, following from that, I might be
able to extract a little more information about that incident
at the Museum."

"Yes, you might," Toby agreed, "and let me be the first
to wish you every success!"

CHAPTER TWENTY

•

The postscript had been duly noted and Alice brought her old school friend round to my dressing room after the morning matinee, although this entailed more inconvenience for them both than I could have foreseen. The old school friend, whose name was Marian, was badly crippled with arthritis and even to hobble so short a distance as that required a painful effort. To make amends, I insisted on her remaining behind, while Alice went off on her own to collect the car.

"I'm afraid that's one department where the organisers fell flat on their faces," I remarked when she had left. "Not half enough parking space, and when you do find one it's usually miles from the point you want to be."

"Well worth it this time, though. I haven't had such a giggle for years and you were absolutely super. We both nearly died when you were taking off that other woman," Marian assured me earnestly, evidently being the type of old school friend who still clung relentlessly to the old school language.

"Of course, Miss Dilloway had seen it before, so I'm afraid she must have been rather bored," I said, not above doing a little fishing, so long as there was half a sprat left in the sea.

"Bored, my foot! It was seeing it before which made her so keen to take me. And I bet you it's the kind of play you could go to half a dozen times and still find something new to enjoy."

"Well, that's very cheering news," I told her, dropping one fishing rod in order to get to work with another. "And I'm so relieved to hear that it doesn't have bad associations for her. I was a bit worried about that because I happen to know that the other occasion was the very last time she saw her sister alive."

"Well, I think that was pretty much an eleventh hour arrangement, wasn't it? And, you see, Alice had already mentioned to me that she was planning this little treat, so she wouldn't have wanted to disappoint me, bless her! Besides . . ."

"Yes?"

"Well, I don't want to speak out of turn, but I don't see how anyone could be all that cut up by Edna's death, do you? Between you and me and the what-have-you, she was a selfish, self-centred old b., if you'll excuse my French, and she treated Alice like dirt."

"But that was only recently, wasn't it? I gather they were devoted to each other in their younger days?"

"Search me!" Marian said blankly. "I can't say I ever noticed much love between them, but then Edna was a year or two older than us and in a higher form. Not all that much higher, I might add. She was a perfect dud at school."

"Not very bright?"

"You can say that again! She didn't give a hoot about getting on, either. The only things that interested her were plastering her face with make-up and dreaming about being a film star."

"Oh, really?"

"Cross my heart. Of course, she wasn't bad looking in those days and it was an absolute craze with her. She'd have spent every waking minute at the pictures, if she could have got away with it."

"But not the theatre?" I suggested sadly.

"Well, not so easy for us girls to come by, of course, but oh yes, she used to squander her pocket money there too. Whoops? There I go again, putting my foot in it! But it was mainly musicals with her, not the kind of worthwhile things you do. Jack now, her first husband, he was very different; ever so keen on music and opera, Gilbert and Sullivan, you name it. Even used to drag Edna to them sometimes. You'd have thought she was going to her execution. Her idea of the theatre was hanging round the stage door, imagining that Ivor Novello had given her a special look, if you know what I mean?"

"Rather like our own dear pop fans of today?"

"That's about it, although I do remember now that she quite fancied her own talents as an actress too. There was one terrible term when she was given the leading part in the upper school play. Scenes from *Cranford*, I think it was; anyway, it got a write up in the local rag and after that there was no holding her."

All this was immensely more interesting and informative than anything I had hoped for, and it was tempting to let the total recall proceed on its own momentum, but I had allowed for a maximum of twenty minutes to elapse before Alice returned with the car. Only three now remained and the vital question had not yet been touched on, so I cut into these reminiscences by saying:

"And I suppose you knew Bella quite well too?"

"Come again!" Marian said blankly. "Bella, did you say? No, I don't remember anyone of that name. Who's Bella, when she's at home?"

"Oh, you know, Mrs. Mortimer's great friend. She was always going on about how marvellous and clever she was. I have an idea she lives in London now, but I always understood she was at the same school as the rest of you."

Marian shook her head: "It's gone, I'm afraid. The old memory's not what it used to be, and I've been out of touch with Edna for years now; ever since her first husband died, in fact. The name Bella mean anything to you, dear?" she added, as Alice entered the room within one minute of her allotted time.

She was in no mood for chatty conversation however, and either did not hear the question or chose to ignore it, her mind being full of the terrible fate which awaited the car at the hands of a prowling traffic warden, if they did not return to it immediately. Sticks, coats and bags were gathered up with all speed and in two minutes they had gone, no further mention of Bella having been made by anyone.

Nevertheless, I was far from feeling that the interview had been a waste of time.

"What about that friend of your grandmother's, Bella something? Did she come to the funeral?"

Rather more hung on the answer this time than in the previous interrogation, because during the interval I had read the whole of Vol. Four and the name had cropped up again, but in a more suggestive and dramatic context.

"No idea."

"But surely, Camilla! I mean, either she was there, or she wasn't there?"

"Too right, Miss Clever! Either she was there, or she wasn't and, since I don't know her from Adam, I've no idea which."

"Not even by sight?"

"No, and never heard of her, what's more. Why are you so interested?"

"No particular reason, only your grandmother mentioned her to me once or twice and I was a bit curious."

"I can't see anything to be curious about in that."

"Well, she sounded rather an unlikely friend for Edna to have had; not as though they had much in common. For example, on one occasion I gather they went to the V. and A. together, and that must have been a novelty, to put it mildly."

"When was that?"

"I'm not sure. Could have been several years ago, come to think of it, but it had stayed very fresh in her memory, which is hardly surprising."

"Well, Tilly would be the one to know the details. You'd better ask her, if it means so much to you."

"I've already done so, but for once she wasn't much help. She has a vague recollection of Edna telling her how she'd spent the morning in some museum in London, but she can't remember when it was or who she'd been there with."

"There you are, then! The whole story was probably pure invention, to prove to everyone how cultured she was, because I can tell you one thing for sure. No one called Bella wrote to condole, or I'd have remembered. It was rather a joke, actually, because Bernard's mother was all for us putting a notice in *The Times*, saying that every letter would be answered personally and all that stuff, but as there weren't more than half a dozen of them, apart from the locals, Ferdy and I both thought it would be rather a waste of money."

All this was related with great insouciance, not a hint of guilty hesitation anywhere and, although I knew her to be capable of deceit when expediency demanded it, I was convinced that she was concealing nothing this time. Indeed, and hardly surprisingly, Camilla's good fortune had already brought a vast improvement in her manners and outlook. The furtive, rabbity expression had largely vanished and it was quite a common sight these days to see her with her mouth shut.

So I was resigned to drawing my second blank and not at all disheartened, believing that a positive answer would have been more damaging to my lovely new theory than a negative one. I must have been half asleep, though, for had I looked so much as one stage ahead, I would surely have seen what a dangerous path I was now treading.

CHAPTER TWENTY-ONE

•

"It is my firm and considered opinion that you may sleep easy in your bed-sitter from now on," I informed Ferdy, still galloping along in my fool's paradise. "The evidence may be all negative, but as far as I'm concerned it's conclusive. You will not be breaking any rules, legal or otherwise, if you burn that unsigned will and forget you ever saw it. You may as well burn this old diary too, while you're about it. The loss to posterity will be negligible."

"What do you mean by negative?" Ferdy enquired, zooming straight to the weakest part of the argument, as was his custom.

"I'll explain that in a minute. A question for you first: did you ever hear her speak of a woman called Bella?"

"No, never."

"I thought as much. If she exists at all, it's most likely under another name. However, that's not particularly important. The point is that there are several references to her in the diary, only one of which concerns us, because it is linked with the subject of the will."

"How come?"

"Actually, it comes almost at the end, in the last entry but one. Unfortunately, it's only dated by the day of the week, but we can narrow it down as much as we need to by the fact that, around the same time, there's mention of the Festival, which was then in preparation and begging for funds, but hadn't yet started."

"Oh yes?"

"What I'm driving at is this, Ferdy: that being the case, it must also have coincided with the early stages of her illness, probably just after her first or second attack; and what I now see clearly is that they had not only caused physical damage, they had also affected what passed for her brain."

"How do you know?"

"Because quite out of the blue and after only one fairly detached allusion to her, she's got her knife stuck into this Bella and is determined to bring her down at all costs. Now, if you think back, Ferdy, you'll remember that the only women who were in any position to do her any injury during that period, when she was virtually cut off from outsiders, were Tilly and Camilla. Bella cannot have been a pseudonym for either of them because we know that they are both accounted for under other labels. There was garrulous old Mattie, you remember, and Greta is unmistakably Camilla. So that leaves the indisputable conclusion that whatever grievance she'd worked up against this Bella must have been imaginary."

"But in what way had she got her knife into her?"

"Ah well, that's what I've been leading up to. Sorry to have laboured it, but it was essential to give you a full picture of the background, if you're to grasp the significance of the passage in question."

Ferdy was now looking at me in a way to suggest that he had small hope of capturing any sort of picture of the foreground, let alone the back, so I said quickly:

"I'll now read a sentence aloud to you, after which I suggest you read it for yourself, so that we can both be absolutely sure that there's nothing to worry about."

Whereupon, I opened Vol. Four, turned to the penultimate page and began as follows:

" *Tuesday. Such a pretty morning, with blue sky abounding, but May's heart was black and heavy within her. It had been a night of nightmares and torments and her first thought on waking was the same one as had lulled her into a fitful sleep. Come what may and no matter who might suffer, Bella should never, never get her evil hands on one*

penny of the money, though she lived to be a hundred.
There was much to be done and it needed thinking out,
but a plan was already beginning to take shape in May's
agile mind.' "

I raised my eyebrows, at the same time handing the
book to Ferdy, who recoiled as though expecting it to
explode in his face. Having made a pretence of reading
the passage I had marked for him, he said unhappily:

"It sounds absolutely dotty, I agree, but would you say
it actually proved that she was out of her mind?"

"Wouldn't you?"

"Well, no, not necessarily," he admitted. "Sorry if I'm
being thick, Tessa, but I can't see how it actually proves
anything at all. If this was written, like you say, when she
was already ill . . ."

"You can read the evidence for yourself, if you don't
believe me."

"Of course I believe you, don't be daft! I was only going
to say that if it was written then, well, I agree with you
that, the way we were all keeping a watch on her, this
Bella couldn't possibly have moved in close enough to
nobble her; but it still doesn't have to have been straight
fantasy on Edna's part. There could have been a letter, or
phone call, or something like that."

"Yes, there could, I agree. Personally, I'm of the opinion that if there had been Tilly would have known about
it, but all that is completely and utterly beside the point."

"Oh, is it?" Ferdy asked, looking more baffled than
ever.

"Yes, it certainly is because all that really matters is that
this Bella, whoever she was, didn't benefit under the old
will, any more than she lost out in the new one. The only
people to do that, apart from yourself, were her sister
Alice and Tilly and Camilla, and so therefore, indirectly
Bernard, I suppose. Now, Bella came on the scene only
comparatively recently, so we know she's not included
among that lot and so what are we worrying about? Edna's
mind must have started to crack as soon as she had her
first attack, perhaps even before. Unfortunately, she was
such an idiot in many ways that nobody noticed much

difference; but by the time she got the idea of altering her will she must have deteriorated so badly that she could no longer distinguish between fact and fantasy, real people and phantoms. Got it?"

"Yes, I think so. I think I do begin to understand now, and thanks a lot, Tessa. It all seems a bit more straightforward now you've explained it and I'd never have got to the starting post on my own. I knew you'd be able to sort it out, if anyone could."

Not for the first time, Ferdy's innocent faith in my omnipotence slightly blemished the triumph of having won the battle so easily, but I was able to console myself with the reflection that at least I had told him no lies and that it was hardly my fault if he did not choose to look beyond the bare facts. If it had not occurred to him to wonder about the real identity of Bella, or to ask himself in what manner Edna might have struck at her through one of the heirs of the original will, the onus was not on me to put such questions into his head.

CHAPTER TWENTY-TWO

•

1

At one stage during my undercover investigations, when
Camilla had figured prominently among the runners in the
impersonation stakes, it had occurred to others as well as
myself that her engagement to Bernard had resulted from
expediency, rather than true love, as a means of ingratiating herself with Edna, and later on this theory had been
strengthened by some remarks which Helena had let fall,
indicating that she had reached a similar conclusion via a
somewhat different route.

However, we had obviously misjudged her, for, as Marge
pointed out while we watched the preliminaries to the St.
Leger, which she and Vi had kindly invited me to view on
their television, one of the bonuses of Camilla's new security had been the cessation of hostilities between her and
her prospective mother-in-law.

"Funny thing about that girl, you know," Marge observed in thoughtful tones. "I always used to say that in
many ways she and Edna were so alike that they could just
as well have been blood relations. Now that Edna's no
longer with us, she seems to be falling into Helena's orbit
in exactly the same way. It even applies to her clothes,
had you noticed? I'm sure that dress she wore at the
funeral must have been chosen by Helena. It was so much
less bitty than her usual style."

"Perhaps she's fundamentally very unsure of herself?" I

suggested. "She needs someone with a strong character to set the tone for her?"

"Or a stable companion to make the running," Vi said with a suitably equine guffaw.

Due to some hitch or other, the horses on the screen were still ambling round and round near the starting post and the commentator was saying: "And now let's take another look at the betting!" in tones of quiet desperation and for about the fifteenth time.

"What about Robert?" I asked. "Does he approve of Camilla?"

"He does, if Helena tells him to."

"Honestly? As malleable as that? I'm a bit puzzled by Robert. No one ever seems to pay much heed to him and yet he must have some ability to have become a successful solicitor."

"Become, my foot! Stepped straight into his father's shoes, just as Bernard will. He's quite a decent chap, old Robert. I've nothing against him, but he has very little ability and even less guts."

"Kind, though?"

"Oh yes, very, I think; but what makes you say so?"

"Just something I heard from Tilly. Apparently, he spent a lot of time taking the vacuum cleaner apart for her one evening, when he was all togged up to go out to dinner."

"What an extraordinary thing to do!"

"Just what I said, but I gather he and Helena called in at Farndale on their way to the Mayor's Ball and he got down to work without a murmur."

"Then it was all Helena's doing, you may be sure. She has everyone's best interest at heart, but she'd have Robert unblocking the gutters on a freezing night in January, in his pyjamas, if her conscience dictated it; and I daresay Camilla will end up just the same. She'll be dangling Bernard up and down on a string, for his own good, in no time at all. Still, he'll only be exchanging one domineering female for another and I daresay he takes after his father in that way too; never quite comfortable without some bossy woman at his elbow, telling him what to do."

"I wouldn't bet on that," Vi said. "Bernard may be on

the dim side and he's certainly toed Mum's line up till
now; but he's a deep one too, with a lot of Helena in him,
and I wouldn't bank on Camilla having quite such an easy
run. And quiet now, please, both of you!" she added,
holding up a commanding hand, as the picture switched
back to the scene by the stalls and the commentator
announced with a sob of relief that they were all safely in
now.

It was premature, however, for a second later the cam-
era tracked back twenty yards to show a strange hooded
beast by the name of Shed A Light being propelled forci-
bly towards the last empty stall by two men pulling at one
end and three more pushing from behind.

"Is it too late to put a bet on?" I asked, fascinated by
this spectacle.

"Yes, of course, far too late," Vi said, as the gates swung
open and runners and riders streamed out over the wide
green ribbon of turf.

2

"Just as well, of course," I admitted later to Toby. "Either
poor old Shed A Light never made it into the stalls, or if
she did she was under the impression that that was the
sole object of the outing because she was never mentioned
again. Marge backed the winner, I need hardly tell you,
and that was purely because its owner had the same
surname as her old Nannie, which doesn't strike me as
being an any more logical reason than mine. But there you
are! She won and I would have lost, which probably does
prove that she's the expert in her own peculiar field."

"Perhaps because she's consistent? However unsound
her reasoning, at least it doesn't hop about. Unlike you,
she would not back a horse simply because it was patently
unfitted to race at all and was bored to tears by the whole
business. Presumably, the one whose owner was named
after Nannie had as good a chance as any, but you were
really loading the dice against yourself."

"No, you don't understand, Toby. It had nothing to do

with the horse's behaviour, although it may surprise you to learn that the temperamental kind often go like the wind when they start; it was simply because it reminded me of Camilla."

"Oh yes, that explains everything."

"Not only because of the stubborn way it was behaving, but also, you see, we'd been talking about her and her chameleon type personality and when the commentator started going on about this naughty little filly, Shed A Light, I had the strange sensation that he was speaking confidentially to me. I still had Camilla on my mind and it came to me in a flash."

"What did, for heaven's sake?"

"This mental picture of her on the night of Edna's death. It was the horse's name which tied the whole thing up for me, you see?"

"No, of course I don't see."

"In this picture of her which leapt into my mind, she was sitting in Edna's room and the only shaft of light came from a table lamp on the little writing desk under the window which faces the bed. Now do you follow me?"

"Absolutely not one inch."

"Right, then we'll go back and start at the beginning. You remember how, when Camilla discovered that Edna was dead, she went into tearing hysterics?"

"Yes."

"And the rather curious story she told of having fallen asleep and woken up to find the door shut, and when she went to investigate she heard the click of the front door? You remember that?"

"Vaguely."

"And then, when she eventually went back to Edna, she found her dead and went ranting round the house, shrieking that it was all her fault?"

"That I do remember; it made quite an impression."

"Then I wish you'd said so at the time, Toby. I discounted it, as an extra touch of the histrionics, but it would have saved endless delay if I'd taken her seriously."

"Delay in what?"

"Arriving at the truth. Yes, really, that old thing! You see, I'm now very positive that she was directly responsible for Edna's death, although not at all in the way she described it."

"Do go on! I admit to being agog!"

Nothing loth, to borrow an expression which Edna had made frequent use of in her diary, I said:

"Then first picture the scene: there are two windows and under the smaller one which faces the bed, is this little old-fashioned writing table, with lots of drawers and pigeon holes. Now, we know Camilla to be of a somewhat volatile temperament and, although she was only to be on duty for three hours, she admitted that it stretched ahead like an eternity, so what more understandable if the sight of the little desk seemed like an invitation to relieve the tedium in the most practical of all ways?"

"With a bit of snooping?"

"Exactly! Having first closed the door, of course. My belief is that, having ascertained that the patient was still in a torpor, she set to work to make a thorough search, but unfortunately the room would then have been pitch dark and it would have been necessary to switch on the table lamp."

"Yes, I suppose it would."

"I say 'unfortunately' because, as Tilly had explained to me on an earlier occasion, the one thing which really disturbed and upset Edna was any form of direct light."

"Wouldn't Camilla have been warned about that too?"

"She might not have listened and, if she had, she could still have thought Tilly was fussing unnecessarily. She always thinks she knows better than anyone else, only this time she was wrong and Tilly was right."

"And the old lady woke up in a fit and . . . ?"

"Probably died of fury and frustration, guessing in a flash what was going on. Presumably, Camilla realised almost at once what she had brought about, lost her head completely and went rushing out to the landing, scream-ing her head off. I'd say that at this point the hysterics were perfectly genuine. It was only later, when her brain began to function again, that she realised she was on to a good thing and kept the act going. For instance, that extraordinary scene she made about returning alone to

Edna's room, before the doctor arrived, to say her last goodbyes in private! Can you imagine anything more freakish or morbid? Or less in character, come to that! Camilla was the one who used to pass out cold at least once in every game of Sardines. So you can guess what I believe was the real purpose behind that touching little exercise?"

"To tidy up some loose ends, I suppose?"

"Right first time. Honestly, Toby, it's quite a pleasure talking to you when you're in this mood. Naturally, when that cunning little brain got back on the rails again, it relayed the message that five minutes alone in Edna's room was absolutely essential to ensure that the desk was neat and tidy, the light off and not one shred of evidence to show that she had ever been near it."

"Yes, and I agree that your picture of events is slightly more plausible than hers, but it is all based on the premise that she did sit down and go through the desk when she had the chance, and plausible is not enough. For a start, what possible interest could it have had for her?"

"The new will, of course, which she was hoping to find. Either Edna had taunted her with it, or she'd got wind of it some other way; through Tilly, maybe."

"And if she'd found it?"

"Would have destroyed it, I'm willing to bet. Even if her grandmother had survived, she was unlikely to have regained her full mental faculties and if she'd started maundering on about a missing will nobody would have paid much attention. So there'd have been practically no risk in it for Camilla and, you see, Toby, she had no means of knowing that the will was still unsigned and therefore invalid."

"Yes, I do admit that it all hangs together very tidily, but it seems to me that you could still be doing her an injustice. What evidence is there, really, that she knew of the will's existence? If you can give me a convincing answer to that one, I promise not to argue any more."

"It's a deal then, and this time I can flout you because I have a witness."

"Flout away! Who is it?"

"Ferdy."

"Oh, him!"

"Needless to say, he doesn't realise it. He has the type of mind that can only encompass one fact at a time. Cause and effect are beyond his scope, but the inference was perfectly plain to me."

"I don't feel very flouted yet."

"You will, though, because he told me that, as joint executors, he and Camilla had the job of sorting out Edna's papers and correspondence and Camilla not only took it on willingly, she refused to let anyone help her. Now, you know I'm not making it up or being spiteful when I say that in the ordinary way she would have thrown a chore of that kind straight over to Tilly, or indeed anyone else who would take it off her hands, but this time when Tilly offered to weigh in she was turned down flat. Moreover, Camilla reserved all the hardest and most tedious part for herself, sending Ferdy off to play about with his father's papers in the library, in the entirely false belief that no harm could come from that. And another thing: Ferdy told me that she attacked her end of the job like a bat out of hell. It amused him because it was so unlike her, but he never attributed all that frenzied activity to an ulterior motive and, so far as I know, he still hasn't. He thought she might be hoping to turn up some cash, but I think it's much more likely that it was the new will, which she'd tried and failed to find on the night of Edna's death, don't you?"

"Yes," Toby agreed. "I promised you I was ready to be convinced and now you've succeeded. My only regret is that, however beautiful this new truth you've unearthed may be, it still brings you no nearer to solving what I might describe as your primary case."

"Oh, never mind that! Everything which is not a step backwards must be counted as a forward one. There is no such thing as standing still in this game and, if you can only collect enough data on all the characters concerned, you are bound to come up with the solution in the end. Our best bet is to sit back and await developments, for I have a strange feeling that somewhere out there," I announced grandly, waving a hand in the general direction of Farndale, "things are now beginning to hot up."

CHAPTER TWENTY-THREE

•

Annoyingly enough, it was not at all easy to reconcile the next development, when it did come and which happened to be only an hour or two later, with these airy predictions. On the face of it, it was neither a step forward, nor a step backwards. It was not even a marking time, but more of a step sideways and this inconclusive element extended to the development itself, an isolated context. As anonymous letters go, it was innocuous almost to the point of benevolence and yet, given the fact that I had undeniably been traveling around stirring up a little mud here and there, the implications were not entirely pleasant.

Taking this factor into account, I soon reached the decision that my best bet was to hand the letter over to the police with the least possible delay, a policy which was made all the easier to implement by the fact that Robin, back from his northern conference, had arranged to join us at Roakes Common for the last weekend of the Festival and was due at any moment.

It was a short letter, typewritten on a single page of lined paper, perforated at the top and obviously torn from a shorthand notebook. The text was as follows:

"You are strongly advised to leave this place at once. This message is sent to you for your own good. So long as you remain here your life and everything you value may be in danger." There was no signature.

"You'd think they might have signed it 'Well Wisher',"

I complained. "There would seem to be a case for it here."

"I wouldn't be too confident of that," Robin replied. He was treating the matter more seriously than I had anticipated and next surprised me by asking whether there was a typewriter at Farndale.

"Certainly, there is. A clumsy old iron thing about the size of a tank, which Tilly has to make do with. It lives in the old dressing room, where she keeps all her needle-work and it takes two strong men to push the carriage back. Camilla and I used to play about on it when we were children and it was antiquated even in those days."

"Has she got one of her own now? A portable, for instance?"

"May have, I've really no idea. Why? You surely don't imagine that Camilla would be considerate enough to send me a friendly warning if my life was in danger?"

"Maybe not, but to my inexpert eye this message doesn't look as though it had been typed on such an old-fashioned machine and I was trying to eliminate the possibilities. Besides, as I mentioned before, we don't know exactly how friendly the warning was intended to be. The kindly nudge of to-day can become the knife in the back tomorrow. Have you kept the envelope?"

It was an ordinary manilla one, postmarked Storhampton on the previous day and addressed to Miss T. Crichton.

"What does that suggest to you?" Robin asked, when he had remarked on the fact.

"Nothing at all. What does it suggest to you?"

"Several things. One that the sender might be some relatively harmless crackpot, dedicated to stamping out actresses and who only knows you by your stage name. Alternatively, someone who has known you all your life as Miss T. Crichton, still thinks of you in that guise and hasn't caught up with the fact that you are now Mrs. R. Price."

"Well, that's not much help, is it? It strikes me that practically everyone for miles around either only knows me by my stage name or has known me all my life."

"With one notable exception?"

"Yes," I agreed, thinking it over, "with one notable exception. And her letter was certainly addressed to Miss T. Crichton. On the other hand, that one wasn't typed, so it doesn't get us any further."

"How did she react when you asked her about Bella?"

"I didn't need to ask her. Marian did it for me, and I couldn't say for sure that Alice heard her. She was in a high state of panic about having to abandon the car in a vulnerable spot, where a thousand wardens waited to pounce. It could have been genuine; you know what a flap some people get into over that kind of thing? And poor old Marian being such a slow mover must have exacerbated the situation. However, I wasn't hanging on her answer because Marian had already told me all I needed to know."

"About Bella?"

"Well, not specifically, but she put me on the right track. Thinking about it afterwards, it came to me that she'd provided the key to the whole puzzle and the amazing thing was that she'd no idea she'd done it, or even that the puzzle existed."

"So what next? I hope you don't intend to go around using this key to unlock a lot more doors with awkward questions. I've already warned you about the pickle that could land you in."

"No, nothing like that. There's no more need for questions because the answers are all up here in my head, if only I could dig them out."

"Well, at the risk of repeating myself, do take care not to dig them out in the wrong company."

"Why are you so alarmist, Robin? We both know that if a crime has been committed it is not one for which the guilty person could ever be brought to trial."

"That's true, so far as it goes," he admitted gloomily, "but thanks to your interference it may not stop there. It's an occupational disease, I daresay, or perhaps I'm naturally pessimistic, but I always get jumpy when the anonymous letters start to roll in."

"Cheer up!" I said. "Stop jumping and concentrate on

the positive. You're here now, to keep matters in check; Toby and Mrs. Parkes, between them, are concocting a splendid dinner for us and we're to have fireworks on the river to-morrow night. So what have we got to worry about?"

"Nothing in the world, I suppose; unless it rains."

CHAPTER TWENTY-FOUR

•

There was one contingency, however, which neither of us could have foreseen, but which was destined to have far more widespread and catastrophic results than a little rain falling on the fireworks, and this was the strange and unprecedented behaviour of Bernard Plowman.

There had been one or two rumblings along the way, starting as far back as my lunch with Helena, in which she had confided her misgivings about the curious relationship between her son and Camilla, and the most recent of all having been perpetrated by Marge, when she attributed Bernard with hidden depths, which might augur badly for the future; but the first hint of serious trouble came from Tilly on Saturday morning.

She was standing outside a bank in Storhampton's Market Place when I met her, looking harassed and aggrieved, which was a near miracle in itself, although she greeted me in her usual kindly fashion.

"You're out early, Tessa dear!"

"I know, but Toby lumbered me with the weekend shopping and it's a nightmare these days finding somewhere to park, unless you get here practically as dawn breaks."

"Don't speak of it! The whole town seems to have gone off its head with this Festival. I shall be thankful when it's over and we can go back to normal. Do you know, I've been standing outside this place ever since half past nine and they still haven't opened. Disgraceful, I call it."

"And the awful thing is," I told her, "you've got another forty-seven hours and fifty minutes to go."

She still didn't get it, so I said: "The banks don't open on Saturdays."

Whereupon, she first looked defensive, as though suspecting me of insubordination, then flushed scarlet, as her eyes brimmed with tears of exasperation, finally bursting out in a poor imitation of her normal cheerful manner:

"Oh, what a muggins! You're quite right, my dear. Now, what on earth made me forget a thing like that? It must be years since we had these new opening times and you'd think I'd be used to it now. Ah well, anno domini, I suppose."

"Nonsense, Tilly! We all have these occasional lapses. I frequently forget my own telephone number; and you've had a lot to cope with recently."

"That's true enough and now I've given myself another headache, haven't I? How on earth am I going to lay my hands on some cash for the weekend?"

"No problem at all. I've got some I can lend you and if it's not enough we can rustle up some more. Come across the road and have some coffee while we plan the strategy."

"Well, that's a nice thought, but what about your shopping dear? I don't want to hold you up, you know. There's been enough time wasted already without . . ."

I allowed her to prattle on in this way, while we skipped through the traffic to the coffee bar on the opposite corner and sat down at a table by the window, believing her to be more than capable of supplying all the arguments and counter arguments and chatting herself back into a good humour, without any assistance from me.

"How much do you need?" I asked, when the flow had subsided to a trickle.

"Oh, five will be plenty, thank you, dear."

"Be honest, now, Tilly! I have a feeling you wouldn't have staggered all the way to the bank just to draw out five pounds."

"That's true, but it will do me very well, all the same.

There are only one or two small things I must get today and all the rest can wait till Monday."

"All what rest?"

For a moment, to judge by her expression, she was tempted to remind me that curiosity killed the cat, but must have then have recollected that I was no longer nine years old, for she replied in a faintly embarrassed way, as though she were now the child:

"Well, I had it in mind to buy one of those long playing records, but since I really have no idea what they cost I was afraid it might sound silly to ask to pay by cheque."

"It won't cost as much as five pounds, if that's what's worrying you. Have you got the right kind of player for it?"

"What? Oh, you mean gramophone. Good heavens, no, what would I want with a contraption like that? I'm not buying this for myself."

"Oh, a present then?"

"That's right. For Camilla. I happen to know the name of one she's particularly keen on. One of those groups. Dirty Dick, it's called, although there are actually four of them, I gather."

"Why? It's not her birthday."

"I know that, dear. She was born in March. Her grand-father used to give her one pearl for every year of her age. The idea was that when she was eighteen they'd all be strung together to make a necklace. Unfortunately, he died before there were quite enough for that."

"So why give her a present if it's not her birthday?"

"Ah well, you see, she's a little bit down in the dumps, poor child. Sometimes an unexpected treat does wonders to cheer her up."

"What's the trouble? Lovers' tiff?"

"Not that I know of," Tilly said primly. "And I should say it's most unlikely. What quaint ideas you get in that old head of yours, Tessa! No, she's just rather run down and depressed and I can't seem to shake her out of it. I've suggested all sorts of little jobs to occupy her, or even take a book out in the garden now we've got this lovely weather, but no; all she ever wants to do is sit in her room and

listen to records. Of course, she's at a loose end, now they
don't need her any more to help with the Festival, and I
expect she misses her Grannie, poor dear!"

This was too much to take, even from Tilly, and I had
difficulty in suppressing the somewhat brusque expletive
which her words provoked. As though taking it as uttered,
though, Tilly said defensively:

"Oh, you may laugh, and I know they didn't always hit
it off, those two, but it's a funny thing, Tessa. You're too
young to understand this, but when you've been used to a
person almost all your life you do feel a dreadful sense of
loss when they go, you can say what you like. It's just the
same with me. Mrs. Mortimer could be very trying at
times, don't I know? But I still can't take it in that she's
dead. I keep expecting her to walk in the room and start
complaining about something and then, when I remember
that I'll never see her again or hear her grumble about
anything ever again, I get quite a pang, I really do."

"But it's different for you, Tilly. You didn't actively
dislike her. You're incapable of disliking anyone."

"You don't understand, dear. That's not surprising and I
trust it will be many, many years before you have this sort
of experience in your own life, but if you ever do you'll
find it's no help to remember the bad things about people
when they're dead, or the times when you hated them. It
only makes matters worse. Then you've got your own
remorse to cope with, on top of all the other."

"Yes, I can imagine, and I suppose that's what's bugging
Camilla now?"

"Well, of course it is, dear. We all know that there were
times when she resented her grandmother and that she had
good reason to; but now she's regretting that she didn't try
harder to be patient, specially since she's been left all this
money and realises Mrs. Mortimer can't have thought half
so badly of her as she liked to make out. It's quite a
normal reaction and it will pass in time, but the trouble
with Camilla is that she will go to such extremes. Just now
she's managed to work herself up into such a morbid state
that I feel it's almost unhealthy, to be honest with you."

"Morbid in what way?"

"Well, harping on death all the time. Keeps asking me if I think Mrs. Mortimer knew she was dying and if she was frightened by it; and whether I've ever thought about my own death and how I'll face it when it comes, and all this sort of thing. On and on until I could shake her."

"Yes, it must be intensely boring, but, as you say, she's always been a martyr to her moods and I daresay this one will fade just as quickly as all the others."

"It can't fade too quickly for me, I can tell you that much, but I'm not so optimistic. This one should have run its course already. It came on, oh must be almost three weeks back, when she insisted on making a will. Did you ever hear of such a thing? Well, I know it's sensible and practical and all that, now that she's got so much to leave, but really, for a girl of her age! Don't you call that morbid?"

"Did you tell her so?"

"No, I didn't. Like a fool, I encouraged her. I can see my mistake now, but just between you and me, Tessa, I took it as one of those little self-dramatising heroics that Camilla still hasn't quite grown out of, and I thought once she'd got that off her chest she'd be all right again and settle back into her old self. It was stupid of me not to twig that this one went much deeper, because ever since then she's been getting worse than ever."

"What about Bernard? Can't he snap her out of it?"

"Bernard's not here at present, more's the pity! He's had to go to Scotland for a few days. They've got a rich client who inherited a big estate up there. He's much too grand to come south to see his lawyers nowadays, so the partners have to take it in turns to visit him every so often in his castle. At least, they're supposed to take it in turns, but Bernard being the only bachelor, it usually falls to him."

"When is he coming back?"

"Well, that's another thing. He was to have caught the early plane this morning, so as he could take Camilla to the fireworks tonight, but he telephoned to say he couldn't manage it. Reading between the lines, it sounded as though the old man was making a great fuss about keeping him up there for the weekend. Helena sees that as a big feather in his cap and I daresay it is, but Camilla said he sounded as cross as two sticks about it, and of course she's most dreadfully disappointed, poor girl."

"How about Ferdy, then? Can't he take her to the fireworks?"

"Old Ferdy's on the loose too, bless his heart! There's a big race at Ascot this afternoon. To let you in on a little secret, Tessa, he had to borrow the money to get there, which is why I'm so short. Still, he's promised to try and get back this evening."

"Let's just hope he's had the foresight to buy a return ticket!"

"Yes, that's a point, isn't it? I know he'll do his best, dear old boy, but somehow or other things don't always turn out quite right for him. I suppose . . . ?"

"What?"

"I suppose I shouldn't ask this, but if anything should happen that Ferdy couldn't be here in time, you'll be going with Robin and Mr. Crichton, won't you? I don't suppose you'd be a dear and take Camilla along? So much more fun for her than being with an old stick like me."

It was never easy to oppose Tilly. That subtle blend of childlike trust and governess authority had crushed my resistance more often than I could count, but this time I knew that surrender would only leave me with an even more formidable battle to wage and, putting it diplomatically, I said:

"If it were just Robin and me, I'd say yes like a shot, but you know how it is, Tilly? Toby and Camilla have never been able to hit it off. They bring out the worst in each other and I honestly don't think it would make a very jolly evening for her, if he was in one of his snappy moods."

Tilly neither argued nor acquiesced, but bowed her head in a resigned kind of way, as though one more disappointment were only to be expected. Shortly afterwards she gathered up her belongings and bustled out to the street, leaving me with the uncomfortable sensation of having betrayed the childike trust, punched several holes in the governessy authority and thrown in quite a dollop of 'et tu, Brute!' as well.

I looked in at the record shop a few minutes later, meaning to repair some of the damage to my self-esteem with assurances that we would look out for her and Camilla at the fireworks and maybe all meet up for a drink at some point, but she was not there and I was stuck with my guilty conscience for at least another two hours.

CHAPTER TWENTY-FIVE

•

1

At five forty-five that evening I presented myself at the Town Hall basement, decked out in accordance with my sponsors' instructions, in actressy type clothes and make-up, the draw for the raffle having been scheduled for six p.m.

There were not more than fifty people present and the prize was won by a frail looking, elderly man, who wisely donated it to be auctioned off with the others. He then pushed his luck by opening the bidding at five pounds and three minutes later was writing out a cheque, looking understandably more frail and elderly than before.

By this point the local auctioneer was firmly in the saddle and when one or two more works of art had come under his hammer Marge, who had been practically squeaking with suppressed excitement, muttered to Vi that she supposed it would be all right if the three of us now drifted away. Vi nodded and led the way up the stone staircase into the daylight.

"Thank you, Tessa," she said, "you did that very gracefully. And now, where's your car?"

"Nowhere," I replied. "That is, Robin is using it this afternoon to play golf. It's all right though because he's going to pick me up at my local at seven, so I've heaps of time to walk."

"Where's your local?"

"Jolly Angler. Opposite the Chapel."

"We may as well deliver you there," Marge said in an

over-casual voice. "I wouldn't mind a drink myself and our car's right here in front of us. We get special parking privileges when we're on Festival business."

"I didn't," I remarked, as we sped down the temporarily deserted High Street.

"Didn't what?" Vi demanded.

"Get special parking privileges. I was on Festival business for two and a half weeks, not counting rehearsals, and nobody offered any to me."

"Have you heard the news?" Marge asked, unable to contain herself any longer.

"What news?"

"You were getting paid for it, that's the difference. There's still some justice left in the world," Vi said, gliding to a halt on a double yellow line.

"Oh, is that the news?" I enquired, following them into the Starboard Lounge.

Ferdy was already there, seated at the bar. He normally patronised the humbler saloon next door, so I concluded that the big race at Ascot had been won by the right horse.

"Have a drink!" he suggested when I stopped to congratulate him, while Vi and Marge, with a good deal of wrangling and chopping and changing, were installing themselves at a corner table.

"No, thanks. As you see, I am not alone."

"Heard the news?"

"That seems to be to-night's password. Where did yours come from?"

"Tilly. I just rang up to let her know I was back. She sounded paranoiac. Ranting on and on until the pips had gone about three times."

"What about?"

Vi, now on her feet again, was bearing down on us and Ferdy leant sideways and spoke three words in my ear.

"Two scotch, please! One with a dash!" Vi said, rapping out her commands to the barman. "What about you, Tessa?"

"Gin and tonic, please!"

"And one gin and tonic! Ferdy?"

"Oh well, thank you very much. I'll have half a bitter, if that's okay?"

"Aren't you coming to join us?"

"It's awfully kind of you, but I don't think I'd better. Tilly's coming to collect me, you see. She's not allowed to leave the car outside and she wasn't sure when she'd be able to make it, so I have to keep an eye on the road."

"Why not give her a ring?" I suggested, "and, if she hasn't already left, tell her not to bother. Robin will be here in a minute and we can drive you home."

"Oh, really? Well, okay then," he said, clambering slowly down from his stool. "The only thing is . . ."

"I know," I said, fishing in my purse. "Here's some change for the call box."

It was mean and ungrateful, I know, after all their kindness, but it is no use pretending. The temptation was too much to resist and I did not even try very hard:

"Here's to you!" I said, raising my glass to each of them in turn. "And I can't wait to hear your news. But before you begin on that, did you know that Bernard had eloped?"

2

Such pulling of the carpet from under the feet of my dear friends had not been purely for laughs, for it had occurred to me that, even allowing for Ferdy's well known incompetence with mechanical objects, I could not depend on a delay of more than five or six minutes in which to conclude his business on the telephone and rejoin the party. At this point Vi and Marge would both have instantly clammed up and started talking about the ground conditions at Ascot, very likely just as the climax of the story was in sight. Furthermore, it was probable, if not certain, that they had heard of Bernard's elopement from Helena, whose whitewashed account intrigued me far less than the unembroidered version from Farndale. There was also the fact that I had set matters up in such a way that Robin would be able to hear it too, and from the beginning, which in fact was exactly how it turned out.

Ferdy's absence exceeded the time I had allowed for it by approximately thirty seconds and he and Robin came into the Starboard Lounge together. Robin, who was also in an advanced state of nervous tension about the parking hazards, or pretending to be, refused a drink and, after a flurry of goodbyes and promises to look out for each other at the fireworks, we bundled into the car and set off for Farndale.

Not that I had hoped for much enlightenment from Ferdy, who, besides taking so long to reach the point of any subject unconnected with horse racing, was not disposed to treat this new disaster very seriously. Certainly, it had its comical side, as Robin pointed out:

"Elopement seems such an old-fashioned word. It conjures up pictures of dashing young blades in top hats, clinging to ladders, while young ladies make a perilous descent from their bedroom windows; and coach and horses thundering through the night to Gretna Green. Are you sure you've got it right, Ferdy?"

"I'm only repeating what Tilly told me. It was her word, not mine."

"Did she happen to mention who he'd eloped with?" I asked.

"Some woman, I gather."

"Well, that's a comfort, I suppose."

"Not anyone very young is what I mean. Tilly kept talking about this scheming woman."

"I think perhaps all females become women when they start to scheme," Robin suggested. "Scheming girl doesn't carry quite the same venom."

"I daresay this one really is a woman though, because she's got a husband already, and some children. Tilly kept asking me how she could be so wicked as to abandon those poor little innocent children. As though I could tell her!"

All this was substantially true, as we discovered on reaching the house a few minutes later. Tilly came tearing out, distraught and dishevelled, to thank us for bringing Ferdy

home and to offer us a drink. The invitation was not
couched in very pressing terms and Robin was already
making deprecating noises before it was out, but, fortunately for me, there was another car parked by the front
door, and at such an awkward angle that it had left no
space for ours to turn in.

"That's Helena's," Tilly explained. "I'm afraid she was
in a hurry and the difficulty is that she's upstairs, talking
to Camilla. I'd rather not disturb them, if it can be avoided,
not for another five minutes anyway, so do come in and sit
down for a minute and then I'll see what can be done
about getting her to move it."

Once inside, however, it quickly became a problem of
how to get out again, for, having mopped her eyes and
apologised about four times for being such an old goose,
the combination of sympathetic murmurs from Robin and
a stiff whisky from Ferdy unloosed the floodgates and the
five minutes had doubled before the story brought her
round to Helena again. The gist of it was as follows:

Bernard had evidently been less than candid in implying that he was prolonging his visit at the request of his
host because, in fact, he had already left the castle when
he telephoned and, in passing the judgement that he was
as cross as two sticks Camilla must have mistaken vexation
for embarrassment. A letter to his parents, already posted
by then, had not been delivered until they had left for
their respective offices, which was probably just as well,
for it would not have made very cheerful breakfast time
reading. As a matter of fact, it did not make very cheerful
lunchtime reading either because another way in which
Bernard had deceived everybody was in letting it be understood that he had taken on these trips to Scotland in a
spirit of self-sacrifice, whereas he had actually gone out of
his way to ensure that they fell to him, purely to gratify
personal wishes.

In short, on a previous visit, some two years earlier, he
had met and become passionately attracted to a young
woman named Anthea Sorkorski, who was from a local
family, but married to a Polish hairdresser. Since then
they had corresponded between visits and on one occa-

sion, not long after he became engaged to Camilla, had spent three days together in London, when Anthea was there for a manicuring course, ostensibly to supplement the family income.

However, they had both now decided that they could neither any longer make do with these clandestine meetings, nor give each other up and, for the time being, were living in lodgings in Paisley.

They were confident that Anthea's qualifications would obtain her a well paid job and Bernard, for his part, proposed to invest such capital as he possessed in a small holding and spend his days working on the land. No decision had yet been reached about Anthea's two small children.

Bernard had added that he would be visiting his parents in the near future, although only for long enough to collect his clothes, car and other belongings, and had thought it best to acquaint them of his plans before they met.

There was only one reference to Camilla in all this and Bernard had not expressed himself very clearly on the subject. There was a strong hint that their engagement had been no more than a façade, entered into mainly to placate his parents and her grandmother and to spare them both the continual nagging about settling down with a suitable partner, although whether Camilla had been a party to this arrangement was left in ambiguity.

In any case, she had apparently not been consulted about its termination and it was no surprise to hear that she had taken the news extremely badly and had been in and out of hysterics ever since two o'clock that afternoon.

Poor Tilly, who admittedly did not have very far to go in this direction, was now literally at her wits' end, leaving unfinished sentences hanging in the air, only to take them up again when everyone had forgotten their beginnings. This imposed rather a strain, so it was no surprise either to hear that Camilla had retired to her room and refused to come out. In fact, I considered that for once she had done the sensible thing.

However, to Tilly, for whom lengthy verbal communication was the panacea, if not the cure for all ills, this voluntary confinement ranked as one step away from dangerous melancholia and in desperation she had sent for Helena. It occurred to me in passing that this action did not entirely accord with Alice's description of the power maniac, intent on keeping all the reins in her own hands, particularly as Tilly then added that Helena was so clever and tactful that if there were one person in the world who could buck Camilla up it was she. Furthermore, she must have pitched her May Day call in pretty strong terms because, despite her own worry and chagrin, Helena had responded instantly. After a token reluctance, Camilla had consented to see her and they had now been closeted together for approximately twenty minutes.

Robin considered that this was long enough and, realising that his patience was rapidly running out, I was about to suggest that I should go up and ask Helena to pass her car keys out to me, when she saved me the bother by entering the room in person.

She looked tightlipped and careworn, as was to be expected, but was, as usual, perfectly complacent about her own competent handling of the situation and made the rest of us feel like drunken layabouts, sitting around enjoying ourselves while she battled single-handed through this crisis. So no one was in a strong position to express doubts when she announced that Camilla was now perfectly composed, having accepted Helena's assurance that this was merely a temporary aberration on Bernard's part, that he would soon come to see how foolishly he was behaving and that, whether or not Camilla still wished to marry him after this juvenile escapade, she had a positive duty to throw up her head, square her shoulders and face the world as though nothing had happened; or words to that effect. In order to get this programme off to a dazzling start, she and Robert would be returning in two hours time to collect Camilla and escort her to the fireworks.

She then rounded off this performance by informing us that she was not in the habit of locking up when visiting friends, so it had only been necessary for Robin to release the handbrake of her car and give it a good push.

"I would cheerfully give her a good push," Robin muttered, furious at not having thought of this himself. "Preferably when she's standing on the edge of a cliff."

"Perhaps it's mostly put on?" I suggested as we drove away.

"Put on?" he replied, still smouldering. "Are you joking? It's second nature to her to trample all over people while telling them they're fools to put up with it. Odious woman . . ."

"I wasn't referring to Helena, actually, although I do think you ought to make some allowance for her in these hard times, when all her dreams for the glory and advancement of Bernard lie shattered at her neatly shod feet."

"Serve her bloody well right! Who were you referring to, then?"

"Camilla, of course. I was wondering whether she was putting on an act of being heartbroken, when all the time she's been prepared for this to happen, because she and Bernard had agreed on it from the beginning."

"Why the hell should she bother? Since the engagement of convenience, if that's what it's called, has served its purpose, why go on pretending. Now she's got her money, what's to prevent her being as cynical and cold-blooded as he is?"

"Ah, but it's different for her, isn't it? Bernard may see it in that light, but then he has found and won his only true love and he can afford to be a bit offhand about Camilla's feelings. Furthermore, he's still at the centre of the drama and likely to remain so for weeks to come; whereas all that's left for her is to play the jilted loser, wearing a brave smile, which is not a very rewarding role for anyone, least of all her. Also I have a suspicion that all this heartbreak and tears could be a means of endearing herself to Helena."

"What a fantastic idea! She would have to be off her head! Personally, if I were in her shoes the big, bright consolation in all this would be that I was no longer stuck with Helena as a mother-in-law."

"But you're not in her shoes, are you? And you haven't spent your whole life striving to become someone's only pet lamb."

"How do you know I haven't?"

"Well, perhaps what I really mean is that you've been more successful at it. The only time when Camilla really shone in the Little Lord Fauntleroy part was when she was a tiny child and the sun, moon and stars to her doting grandfather. All that came to an end when he re-married and she's been searching for a substitute ever since. First, she made a brave stab at becoming Tilly's darling angel, which worked fairly well for a time, but inevitably Tilly became disenchanted. She still loved Camilla, but she loved her warts and all, which wasn't any good. Camilla needed uncritical, unqualified worship and nothing less would do. When her grandfather died, I think she set her sights on Edna for a while, practically turning somersaults to transform herself into the dutiful, docile granddaughter, dancing attendance and having this pretty romance with the boy next door."

"You don't think Edna's money was the attraction there?"

"Up to a point, of course. I feel sure she wouldn't have worked so hard on anyone who was penniless, but I'm equally sure that the hunger for popularity came into it as well; unfortunately, she was fighting in a lost cause. There was only room for one adored pet in Edna's life and that was herself."

"Poor girl! What a sad, frustrated picture you have painted!"

"Yes, but there are signs that she's not beaten yet and now I think she's after new prey. Helena is starting to take her under her wing, choose her clothes, give advice on how to behave and goodness knows what else. And Camilla is rising like an eager little trout. Helena, you notice, is now the only one she can bear to have near her, and I predict her going flat out before very long to become ever such a ray of sunshine in that arid, childless life."

"Then, quite honestly, she must be barmy! Helena has about as much capacity for affection as a packet of frozen peas."

"And if you think she's not slightly barmy, you haven't taken in a word I've been saying."

"Far enough over the edge to have played that nasty little trick on her grandmother, if she found she was being rejected?"

"Oh, easily, I'd have said; but I've been forced to rule her out, all the same. The evidence is all against her being involved in that."

"And still no nearer finding out who the joker was? I feel for you, my love, but I suppose even you are prepared to admit defeat now? Whoever got that bright idea, if anyone did, must be congratulated on getting away with it, because it's all over now."

"Bar the shouting," I agreed. "And I daresay we can still depend on Camilla to provide us with a little of that."

CHAPTER TWENTY-SIX

•

The opening round of fireworks had been timed to light up the sky half an hour after sunset, which occurred on that Saturday in July at eight minutes to ten. However, as so frequently happens when these things are left to amateurs, no part of the programme went entirely to plan and the first item was delayed by nearly twenty minutes.

By then, a large and somewhat disorderly crowd had assembled on the Oxfordshire side of the river, where access was free and it was a case of first come first served into the front row, and all the nearby pubs having been granted extensions for the occasion.

In contrast to this merrymaking, the scene on the opposite bank was so sedate as to be almost funereal. The two grandstands, specially erected this and every year for the Regatta, had been left intact for the closing Festival event, the smaller being reserved for the Mayor and Corporation, together with all those who had contributed with their services or financial support, while the seats in the larger had all been sold weeks in advance.

There were two marquees behind the stands, also differing in size and distinguished by similar social nuances, one providing soft drinks and beer, the other champagne. Business was slack in both at the start of the proceedings, since only ticket holders to one or other of the stands were allowed into this enclosure.

Toby usually contrives to arrive late for every public

function, not so much on principle as in the very practical hope that at least part of the proceedings will be over before he gets there, and he and Robin and I were apparently the last to be admitted.

His tactics availed him nothing on this occasion though, because all was as silent as the grave and, furthermore, we were obliged to hover about on the outskirts for several minutes, waiting for the attendant to inspect our tickets. This was because he was engaged in acrimonious exchanges with a group of young people who had been attempting to gain admittance by climbing under the ropes. They had presumably arrived on motor bikes, being bundled up in anoraks and helmets, and it was not easy to sort out the sexes, but, passing the time by making a study of each individual pair of hands, which is the really infallible guide in such cases, I came to the conclusion that they consisted of three boys and two girls, their ages ranging between about fifteen and twenty.

In the meantime, Robin had retreated into the shadows and was wearing the face which told everyone that he was not a policeman, while Toby, who had also removed himself from the unpleasant scene, now returned with the news that if we were to leave at once we stood a good chance of getting away before the rush.

It was not his lucky evening though, because for no discernible reason, the altercation at the gate had abruptly ceased. The tallest of the three boys dropped his cigarette on to the grass with a contemptuous gesture and then turned and strolled away towards the car park. A moment's startled hush descended on his four companions, before they too backed away without a word and fell in behind their leader. Robin emerged from the gloom, stamped out the burning cigarette stub and presented our tickets to the attendant.

"You handled that very cleverly," I said, while he was inspecting them.

"Won't do much good though," he replied sourly. "Silly idea, really, having just this rope to keep people out. It's like an invitation to some of them."

"You mean they'll find another way in?"

"Bound to. Nothing to stop them, is there?"

"Except that I can't imagine why they should bother," Toby objected. "It must be just as easy to see the fireworks on one side of the rope as the other."

"Try explaining that to a crowd like them! They've been round here like flies all evening. Never the same lot twice, mark you, and it's not fireworks they've come for. Wouldn't mind betting there are scores of them hanging round the beer tent by now, and looking for trouble. Thick they may be, but it don't take them long to reason out that I can't be in six places at once."

We tut tutted in solemn tones over this, but not for long because a whooshing, whistling sound sliced the air, followed by a series of sharp cracks like pistol shots and an instant later the sky was filled with slow motion showers of crimson, green and gold. The fireworks had begun.

This opening salvo was greeted by tremendous cheering and handclaps, which were repeated with rapidly diminishing fervour every three or four minutes for the ensuing two hours, petering out completely towards the end, so that the resurgence of applause for the concluding set piece, which depicted members of the Royal Family suspended above the bridge, was obviously inspired less by loyalty than relief that the treat we had all looked forward to for so long was over at last.

Long before this reprieve, numerous people had left their hard wooden seats to stretch their limbs by sauntering around on the grass, or revive themselves in one of the tents, and among the first to go had been Camilla.

She had been sitting in the row in front of ours, flanked on either side by a Plowman, and it had to have been something more urgent than sheer boredom which had driven her away, for she left after only a few minutes, risking and indeed incurring a look of marked disapproval from Helena and obliging Robert to stand up and move aside to let her pass.

Some time after this, during one of the many interminable lulls between bursts of activity, there was a whispered consultation across the empty seat, or rather a whispered monologue from Helena, accompanied by nods and shrugs from Robert, which ended with his getting up and sliding away.

Twitching with envy, Toby made another attempt to put across his theory whereby we might get away before the rush, but Robin and I are made of sterner stuff and there were still no takers. Later still, however, during a subsequent passive interval, Robin did concede that we might at least anticipate the rush to the champagne bar, and the three of us folded our rug and silently crept away. It was then ten minutes to eleven.

We made slow progress to the marquee because many of our Storhampton friends and acquaintances had had the same idea and those who did not hold us up in an exchange of comments about how wonderful it all was and how lucky we were that the rain had kept off yet again, were already lined up in the queue for the bar. The noise and heat inside was already passing toleration point and so, leaving the other two to deal with the business end, I took the rug down towards the river, between the two stands, meaning to stake out a claim to some relatively isolated spot. Vi and Marge were not far away, sensibly equipped with camp chairs and vacuum flasks, as well as one or two other groups of people dotted about, but none that I recognised.

I had not caught a glimpse of Camilla, nor Tilly and Ferdy either, but the guardian of the gate had been correct in his prediction that the motor cycle contingent would find their way into the enclosure, with or without his blessing. However, his hint that they were intent on stirring up trouble had evidently been misplaced. I could see about twenty of them, all herded together in a circle on the grass and, although they had a radio playing and were making a fair amount of noise, they appeared to be perfectly harmless and good humoured.

All, that is, except one. This was a lone wolfer, who had detached himself from the group and was behaving in a distinctly odd, not to say sinister fashion. He came face to face with me, only a few yards from where I was sitting, seeming to have arrived there, in some inexplicable fashion, from underneath the larger of the two stands and his reaction on sighting me was so patently startled and alarmed that I became unnerved as well. Despite the dark curls flowing down over the anorak collar, I felt certain this was a male, but applied the usual test, out of force of habit. This was made easy to do by the fact that the shock of seeing me must have caused him momentarily to forget that the helmet and goggles rendered him totally anonymous and he instinctively raised his right hand, as though to cover his face.

It was then my turn to feel the world spinning upside down and by the time I had got it the right way up again he had turned his back on me and streaked away. Inevitably, that would have been the end of it, had not the organisers come to my aid and chosen this moment to loose off another round of fireworks. For about twenty seconds the scene was brilliantly illuminated, with every face save two turned towards the sky, and I had a clear view of the running figure, halting briefly as he came close to his comrades on the grass and then, to my astonishment, swerving away from them and bolting towards the car park behind the enclosure.

For anyone with a vehicle there was only one way out of there and it was by way of a temporary track which led past the main entrance before winding round to join the road at the point where it narrowed into a bottle-neck approach to the bridge.

In the flash which followed immediately afterwards I saw Robin and Toby, not far off, clutching their bottle and glasses and looking around for me; so I ran up to them, grabbed Robin's arm and gabbled a few words in his ear.

Possibly, he thought I was mad and I can see now that he had good grounds, but he earned my everlasting gratitude for the fifty-second time that year by asking no questions and striding nonchalantly but rapidly towards the gate. The amusing part of it was that I felt sure he imagined he was putting on a very convincing act of an innocent spectator setting off to fetch something from his car, but in fact he had absent mindedly kept hold of the bottle and, as he went along, he was swinging it from his right hand, so that it looked exactly like a truncheon.

Toby, however, did not find this at all funny and was inclined to be churlish, not only about having the spoils thus snatched away, after all he had suffered to win them, but also because this treatment would render the champagne undrinkable.

"Never mind," I said, "we can always go and cadge some off Vi and Marge; and anyway there are more important things at stake than champagne shaking."

"I challenge you to name one!"

"Well, prevention of crime may be among them, although I'm not too confident of that. We may already be too late; but I'll tell you one thing for certain."

"Oh, do!"

"Even if we are too late, this may yet prove to be the unique occasion when the hunt is on before the crime has been discovered."

In a sense, things turned out better than that because, although the criminal was unaware of it, the hunt was indeed up before the crime had been discovered. On the other hand, after it had been there was still some delay in settling the score, since for a time it appeared that no outside agency had been involved and the only violence inflicted by the victim's own hand.

It was daylight before Camilla was found, crushed against an inner arch of the bridge, where her clothing had been caught and held by rusty iron nails, although it was reckoned that she had been drowned some hours earlier. In the ensuing police enquiries some curious admissions were made and unknown facts brought to light, some more startling than others, but all contributing to incontrovertible evidence of suicide.

It was not until the pathologist's report had been made public at the inquest and various other witnesses had spoken up, that sufficient of the truth became known to leave the jury with no alternative but to return a verdict of wilful murder.

CHAPTER TWENTY-SEVEN

•

"It is always as well to take note of such little human oddities as may crop up," I remarked with a touch of complacency. "As I once told you, Robin, however insignificant each may appear on its own, they sometimes add up to a formidable whole. For example, if I had not already noted the fact that he was left-handed, I am sure it would never have occurred to me that it was Bernard concealed inside the motor cyclist disguise. But for that, I daresay the episode would have made no lasting impression and he would now be sunning himself in Scotland, or whatever it is they do there."

"I hate to give credit where credit is due," Toby admitted. "It seems so unenterprising somehow, but I am forced to agree that it was rather perceptive of you to have discovered he was left-handed when, to the best of my knowledge, you only met him once and that was at a race meeting."

"Once was enough," I replied, "and the surroundings immaterial. If you will now both hold out your right hands, I will show you how it is done."

Toby obeyed at once and after a moment Robin, smiling because he had guessed what was coming, followed suit.

"You see?" I explained. "Two right hands, two wrists, no watches! Each of you wears one, of course, but you are both right-handed. A left-handed man does it the other way round. The first and only time I met Bernard he was wearing a very gaudy, expensive looking watch. He was also wearing a very old and dowdy looking hat. He was proud of one, but ashamed of the other and he raised his hand in such an ostentatious manner that I was bound to notice the watch. I also noticed that he was wearing it on his right hand, so there we were!"

"Where?"

"Nowhere at the time, naturally. I understand that roughly one quarter of the population is left-handed, so there was nothing sensational about Bernard being one of them. Nevertheless, it was his undoing because when he appeared so dramatically from underneath the grandstand he made the identical gesture, although it was the reverse of deliberate that time. I happened to be watching his hands most particularly and, as soon as he did that, I hadn't any doubt of his identity, or that he was up to something shady. There was nothing clever about the last bit either. People don't dress up as yobbos and crawl about under grandstands unless they are up to something shady."

"And why was he there, in any case? Wouldn't it have been wiser to have kept away?"

"Well, he had to get back to his bike, didn't he, Toby? He'd have looked rather eccentric without one and, besides, he needed it to get as far away from home territory as possible before worse things than fireworks began to explode and, above all, before he was recognised. Obviously, he would have parked his bike in the least conspicuous place available, which was among a whole lot of others in the car park, but unfortunately the only way back to it would have taken him past the entrance gate and we know that the attendant held a slightly prejudiced view of the goggles and helmet brigade. At the very least, his presence and provenance would have been observed, to the extent that it might have been worth while making a note of the registration number when he went by on the bike two minutes later. By taking pains not to alert him in advance, I expect Bernard hoped to slip through the net."

"Having already lured Camilla down to the river and thrown her in, I take it? What a detestable young man! I have always disliked him and I see now that my instinct was right. Camilla may have been irritating, but she scarcely deserved that."

"As it happened, your view of him erred on the side of charity," Robin said. "The evidence shows that he rowed her upstream for some distance above the bridge and then not only threw her in, but held her under. And he must have spun quite a story, moreover, to have induced her to leave the party and accompany him on such a jaunt."

"If we had only been able to listen in to that telephone call from Scotland," I remarked. "We might have some idea of what kind of story it was. Probably something about having got himself embroiled with the other young woman and needing Camilla's help to get disembroiled again."

"Would she really have fallen for such a fatuous tale?"

"Oh yes, so long as it flattered her vanity, and there's no denying that capering about on moonlight assignations, whatever their purpose, would have seemed a lot more romantic than the role of cast-off glove. If I were to moralise, I should probably say now that people mainly get into trouble through their own weaknesses."

"I hope you won't then, for I should regard it as most inappropriate," Toby said. "I have one or two weaknesses myself, some might say, but I had not envisaged having to pay for them with my life."

"And, in any case, I hadn't intended to moralise this time because it wasn't really her fault that she was murdered. No doubt her vanity and self-deception made the job easier, but a way would have been found somehow. The cards were stacked against her from the start, the stacker in chief, of course, being Helena."

"Implying that she put Bernard up to it?" Robin asked.

"Oh no, nothing so tasteless as that, but she did create the circumstances and she did bring him up to worship money. As we heard at the inquest, Camilla was pregnant and she'd reneged on their agreement by falling in love with him, so was all set to make one hell of a stink if he'd abandoned her, I suppose we can't exactly blame Helena for that, but I don't consider that any of it, on its own, would have been sufficient incentive for murder. The trouble was that, with Camilla dead, Bernard was not only free to marry his Scottish manicurist, but he could do so with a dowry of something up to a hundred thousand pounds, which I feel sure was the driving motive. All that talk of scratching a living off twenty barren acres was just rot. It was the money he was after."

"And you hold Helena responsible for that?"

"Certainly, I do. The minute Edna died Helena set about getting Camilla into her clutches and one of her first moves was to persuade her to make a will. Naturally, since they were about to be married, she left everything to Bernard."

"Are you sure?" Robin asked. "I don't remember anything being said about that at the inquest."

"No, but I bet it will come out at the trial. I happened to hear of it from Tilly. She was quite shocked by what she called the morbidity, so obviously it wasn't she who persuaded Camilla, and that only leaves Helena. To give her her due, I'm sure she genuinely believed at the time that they were going to be married, but that's all I will give her. She was a murderess too, in her own very special cunning way; and Marge was quite right in saying that Bernard took after her. They were two of a kind all right."

"And that didn't come out at the inquest either, so far as I was aware."

"No, she got away with it, but I don't see that we need to tear our hearts out over that. It was a cruel trick to play on silly old Edna, but she didn't gain anything by it and the gods sent her far worse retribution than we could ever have dreamt of."

"How did you catch on that Bella was Helena?" Robin asked.

"There were so many clues from so many different sources that it's hard to know exactly. Helena herself provided quite a number. For such a calculating woman, it was really surprising how often she slipped up. Like, for instance, the brazen way she told me that she knew nothing about these strange and ridiculous hallucinations. She and Tilly were as thick as thieves, so she must have heard about them. The fact that she lied meant nothing much at the time, but it was worth noting; and her second big mistake was much more damning. It was when she was telling me about the hairdressers at Stourbury. Incidentally, I expect they were the people who made up the Edna wig, to Helena's very exact specifications, naturally; although I hadn't an inkling of that when I questioned her. I was simply flying kites, to try either to establish or demolish Tilly's alibi for the afternoon when the first apparition turned up on the race course, and the weird thing was that Helena clutched at it as a chance to provide one for herself. She told me she was having her hair tinted that afternoon but, according to Tilly, she only went in for five minutes to arrange about displaying one of the Festival posters and, by then, I thought I knew which of them was likely to be lying."

"Yes, but that still hasn't answered the question as to how you knew she was Bella."

"Well, there was something faintly familiar about those names Edna invented for her characters. For a long time I couldn't pin it down, but it was actually a kind of cipher and Alice's friend, Marian, finally decoded it for me. She explained that as a girl Edna had been almost neurotically stage and film struck, and also that she'd once played the lead in the school play. Now lend me your pen for a minute, Robin, and I'll give you both another visual exercise."

He did so and I wrote down a list of names in three separate columns, explaining as I went along that the first gave the real names, the second Edna's inventions and the third providing, where necessary, the connecting link. When I had finished it looked like this:

Edna	May	Oliver
Alice	Fay	Faye
Tilly	Mattie	Cranford
Camilla	Greta	Garbo (Camille)
Bernard	George	Shaw
Jack	Benny	
Helena	Bella	Belle Helene

"The first thing to hit me," I said, handing the sheet of paper across to them, "was that Benny wasn't short for Benjamin, it was her private name for her first husband, Jack. After that several other things fell into place, one of them concerning the wicked Fay, who had designs on Jack. When Alice was describing that set up she made it sound as though she and Edna were inseparable, with Jack as the odd man out; but of course it wasn't so at all. Whether justifiably or not, it was Edna who felt she was gradually being pushed into that position, which was why she turned against Alice, as soon as she could afford to, and wouldn't let her within yards of old Benjamin for fear of a repetition. It had nothing to do with Tilly's machinations, as Alice tried to make out. Perhaps it suited her to believe that and I daresay she has now convinced even herself, but in fact I should say that Tilly was largely responsible for bringing them together again at the end of Edna's life. And with all that to build on, I think it was safe to assume that Helena was Bella, don't you? Incidentally, Edna called herself May, but it was she who should really have been named Matilda."

"Why Matilda?"

"Wasn't she the one who acquired such a reputation for not telling the truth that when she shrieked out that the house was on fire they only answered 'Little Liar!', and she was burnt to a cinder? I am now harking back to the occasion when Edna told me she had got the tip to back Bitter Aloes 'through her grand-daughter's fiancé', who was a friend of the trainer. No one believed her, but it was probably a half truth because Bernard told me that Helena did know some people in that world and I expected she went to great pains to get some pretty good information lined up for Edna at that meeting, so as to be reasonably sure of getting her round to the pay-out windows after at least one race."

"What beats me," Toby said, "is how she got away with it so often. I can understand pulling it off once, or even twice. That appearance in the garden, for instance, must have been relatively easy, but I would have expected even simple-minded Edna to catch on eventually."

"Well, I daresay she was getting brain-washed, to some extent, but the fact is that Helena didn't get away with it every time."

"She didn't?"

"Certainly not, and we have Edna's own words to prove it; that never, never, come hell or high water, should wicked Bella get her hands on the money. To me, that states as clearly as anything that she had seen through the plot, right down to the fact that Helena had been using the incident at the V. and A., which had been pure coincidence, to torment her in this way."

"Okay, so I can see that made it necessary to cut Camilla out of her will, but how about Tilly and Ferdy? Why did they have to get the same treatment?"

"She may not always have been quite so dim as she appeared and when she said 'Never' she meant precisely that. Knowing Tilly, one can say that it's extremely unlikely that she'd have walked off with fifty thousand pounds, leaving Camilla penniless. I think most of it would have found its way back to her, and so eventually to Bernard, if not during Tilly's lifetime, certainly on her death. As for Ferdy, a backward child of three could have guessed that any legacy he received would remain in his hands for exactly as long as it took him to sign it all away again."

"It's not that I wish to bring you down exactly," Toby said, "but when I recall how often Robin and I have been pinioned here, listening to you modestly recounting your triumphant progress through the labyrinth of crime, it does give me a faint satisfaction to point out that this time you have taken the wrong turning."

"Oh? . . . Have I? . . . Where?"

"If, as you insist, Edna had penetrated the disguise and knew that it was Helena who had been hounding her in this way, then the element of the unknown, which was the key part of the affair, must have been eliminated. In short, since the ghost had now been reduced to flesh and bones, how could it have subsequently returned to cause a fatal heart attack?"

It was now my turn to grow thoughtful and I said: "I admit you have a point there, Toby, and it is one which had occurred to me too, but I think the circumstances and the grotesquerie of that last episode must cancel it out. You once assured me that if you had looked up and seen yourself walking into the room, you would have dropped dead on the spot, and I honestly believe that even if you had been ninety per cent certain that it was only some malicious person playing a vile trick on you, it would still have given you a nasty turn. Now, put yourself in the place of an elderly woman, already groggy from a series of hideous shocks, don't forget! It's the middle of the night and pitch dark; you don't feel well and you're in a hurry to get to the bathroom; in such a hurry that you don't switch on the light. But when you open the door the bathroom is a blaze of light, which accounted for her deathbed phobia no doubt, and there, sitting on the edge of the bath, let us say, malevolently waiting for you to arrive, is yourself, fully clothed in your own mink coat and your own green velvet turban."

"Well . . . yes . . ." he admitted. "When you put it like that, I must admit it would have struck me as rather strange."

"I am positive that each of us would have keeled over and passed out, just as Edna did."

"How did Helena get in?" Robin asked, as though to seal up every crack in my argument. "Surely not by climbing through the bathroom window with a trunkful of Edna's clothes?"

"No, not at all. She walked in through the front door, after they were all in bed, and she wasn't carrying a thing. Ferdy, who is about as wideawake as a dormouse in January told me that he only discovered that Bernard was spending his nights at Farndale because there was some rumpus over his losing the key and I'm sure we don't need to look very far to guess who'd taken it. Moreover, Helena had already been to the house that evening, on what purported to be an errand of mercy. She came to borrow Tilly's embroidery book. Tilly would have it that this was just an excuse to get Robert there to mend the vacuum cleaner, but of course it was the other way round. The excuse she was looking for was to go upstairs on her own, into the little dressing room, where Tilly keeps all her sewing things and which you'll remember is situated between Edna's bedroom and bathroom. And that's precisely what she did, while Robert and Tilly were busy taking the old machine apart. Incidentally, what a broken reed Robert is! No wonder Vi and Marge despise him! He not only kept Helena informed of all developments in Edna's last will and testament, which I am sure is most unethical, but when she began to lose her nerve all he could think of was to write me an anonymous letter, begging me to get lost. It would be nice to think he had my welfare at heart, and perhaps there was a bit of that too, but I'm afraid the fact is that Helena had learnt from Camilla that I was asking questions about someone called Bella and a certain incident at the V. and A. and was rapidly losing control."

"But Helena went on to the Mayor's Ball that evening," Robin pointed out. "And there was no mink draped over her arm when she left Farndale. At least, presumably one of the others would have noticed if there had been."

"No, of course there wasn't. When she nipped upstairs she went into Edna's bedroom and she did two things. One was to drop an emetic or whatever in the bedside carafe and the other to remove such clothes from the wardrobe as she was going to need later on and bundle them away in the dressing room. It only remained to snatch up the embroidery book and saunter downstairs again. The whole operation needn't have taken her more than three or four minutes. Of course, it was a desperate throw, but then she's always been a desperately ambitious and thwarted woman. Edna was getting stronger every day and it might have been only a matter of hours before the hundred thousand pounds slipped away from her darling Bernard for ever. And she was most ingenious, you know, one has to give her that. Honestly, I think we should look at tomorrow's runners. If there's a horse called Ingenuity, or Scheming Lady, or something like that, it could well be worth a modest plunge."

As it happened, there was nothing quite so apposite as that, but there was one in a novice's race at Newbury

called Greta's Pet, which was a striking enough coincidence to sway the most sceptical and I asked Ferdy to
back it for me. It came fifth and I blame myself entirely. If
I had given closer attention to Marge's system I might
have put my money on the one with the same name as the
very first grown-up play my parents took me to, and this
story would have a different ending. It won by a nose and
it was called Interference.

ABOUT THE AUTHOR

ANNE MORICE is the author of fifteen mystery novels, including most recently *Murder Post-Dated* and *Sleep of Death*. She lives in England.

Share in a publishing event!
Rex Stout's Nero Wolfe returns in

Murder in E Minor
by Robert Goldsborough.

Here are special advance preview chapters from
MURDER IN E MINOR, which will be available
as a Bantam hardcover on April 1, 1986, at
your local bookseller.

1

November, 1977

Nero Wolfe and I have argued for years about whether the client who makes his first visit to us before or after noon is more likely to provide an interesting—and lucrative—case. Wolfe contends that the average person is incapable of making a rational decision, such as hiring him, until he or she has had a minimum of two substantial meals that day. My own feeling is that the caller with the greater potential is the one who has spent the night agonizing, finally realizes at dawn that Wolfe is the answer, and does something about it fast. I'll leave it to you to decide, based on our past experience, which of us has it better pegged.

I'd have been more smug about the timing of Maria Radovich's call that rainy morning if I'd thought there was even one chance in twenty that Wolfe would see her, let alone go back to work. It had been more than two years since Orrie Cather committed suicide—with Wolfe's blessing and mine. At the time, the realization that one of his longtime standbys had murdered three people didn't seem to unhinge Wolfe, but since then I had come to see that the whole business had rocked him pretty good. He would never admit it, of course, with that ego fit for his seventh of a ton, but he was still stung that someone who for years had sat at his table, drunk his liquor, and followed his orders could be a cool and deliberate killer. And even though the D.A. had reinstated both our licenses shortly after Orrie's death, Wolfe had stuck his head in the sand and still hadn't pulled it out. I tried needling him back to work, a tactic that had been successful in the past, but I got stonewalled, to use a word he hates.

"Archie," he would say, looking up from his book, "as I have told you many times, one of your most commendable attributes through the years has been your ability to badger me into working. That former asset is now a liability. You may goad me if you wish, but it is futile. I will not take the bait. And desist using the word 'retired.' I prefer to say that I have withdrawn from practice." And with that, he would return to his book, which currently was a re-reading of *Emma* by Jane Austen.

It wasn't that we did not have opportunities. One well-fixed Larchmont widow offered twenty grand for starters if Wolfe would find out who poisoned her chauffeur, and I couldn't even get him to see her. The murder was never solved, although I leaned toward the live-in maid, who was losing out in a triangle to the gardener's daughter. Then there was the Wall Street money man—you'd know his name right off—who said Wolfe could set his own price if only we'd investigate his son's death. The police and the coroner had called it a suicide, but the father was convinced it was a narcotics-related murder. Wolfe politely but firmly turned the man down in a ten-minute conversation in the office, and the kid's death went on the books as a suicide.

I couldn't even use the money angle to stir him. On some of our last big cases, Wolfe insisted on having the payments spread over a long period, so that a series of checks—some of them biggies—rolled in every month. That, coupled with a bunch of good investments, gave him a cash flow that was easily sufficient to operate the old brownstone on West Thirty-fifth Street near the Hudson that has been home to me for more than half my life. And operating the brownstone doesn't come cheap, because Nero Wolfe has costly tastes. They include my salary as his confidential assistant, errand boy, and—until two years ago—man of action, as well as those of Theodore Horstmann, nurse to the ten thousand orchids Wolfe grows in the plant rooms up on the roof, and Fritz Brenner, on whom I would bet in a cook-off against any other chef in the universe.

I still had the standard chores, such as maintaining the orchid germination records, paying the bills, figuring the taxes, and handling Wolfe's correspondence. But I had lots of free time now, and Wolfe didn't object to a little free-lancing. I did occasional work for Del Bascomb, a first-rate local operative, and also teamed with Saul Panzer on a couple of jobs, including the Masters kidnapping case, which you may have read about. Wolfe went so far as to compliment me on that one, so at least I knew he still read about crime, although he refused to let me talk about it in his presence anymore.

Other than having put his brain in the deep freeze, Wolfe kept his routine pretty much the same as ever: Breakfast on a tray in his room; four hours a day—9 to 11 a.m. and 4 to 6 p.m.—in the plant rooms with Theodore; long conferences with Fritz on menus and food preparation; and the best meals in Manhattan. The rest of the time, he was in his oversized chair behind his desk in the office reading and drinking beer. And refusing to work.

Maria Radovich's call came at nine-ten on Tuesday morning, which meant Wolfe was up with the plants. Fritz was in the kitchen, working on one of Wolfe's favorite lunches, sweetbreads in bechamel sauce and truffles. I answered at my desk, where I was balancing the checkbook.

"Nero Wolfe's residence. Archie Goodwin speaking."

"I need to see Mr. Wolfe—today. May I make an appointment?" It was the voice of a young woman, shaky, and with an accent that seemed familiar to me.

"I'm sorry, but Mr. Wolfe isn't consulting at the present time," I said, repeating a line I had grown to hate.

"Please, it's important that I see him. I think my—"

"Look, Mr. Wolfe isn't seeing any one, honest. I can suggest some agencies if you're looking for a private investigator."

"No, I want Mr. Nero Wolfe. My uncle has spoken of him, and I am sure he would want to help. My uncle knew Mr. Wolfe many years ago in Montenegro, and—"

"Where?" I barked it out.

"In Montenegro. They grew up there together. And now I am frightened about my uncle . . ."

Ever since it became widely known that Wolfe had retired—make that withdrawn from practice—would-be clients had cooked up some dandy stories to try to get him working again. I was on their side, but I knew Wolfe well enough to realize that almost nothing would bring him back to life. This was the first time, though, that anyone had been ingenious enough to come up with a Montenegro angle, and I admire ingenuity.

"I'm sorry to hear that you're scared," I said, "but Mr. Wolfe is pretty hard-hearted. I've got a reputation as a softie, though. How soon can your uncle be here? I'm Mr. Wolfe's confidential assistant, and I'll be glad to see him, Miss . . ."

"Radovich, Maria Radovich. Yes, I recognized your name. My uncle doesn't know I am calling. He would be angry. But I will come right away, if it's all right."

I assured her it was indeed all right and hung up, staring at the open checkbook. It was a long-shot, no question, but if I had anything to lose by talking to her, I couldn't see it. And just maybe, the Montenegro bit was for real. Montenegro, in case you don't know, is a small piece of Yugoslavia, and it's where Wolfe comes from. He still has relatives there; I send checks to three of them every month. But as for old friends, I doubted any were still alive. His closest friend ever, Marko Vukcic, had been murdered years ago, and the upshot was that Wolfe and I went tramping off to the Montenegrin mountains to avenge his death. And although Wolfe was anything but gabby about his past, I figured I knew just about enough to eliminate the possibility of a close comrade popping up. But there's no law against hoping.

I got a good, leisurely look at her through the one-way panel in the front door as she stood in the drizzle ringing our bell. Dark-haired, dark-eyed, and slender, she had a touch of Mia Farrow in her face. And like Farrow in several of her roles, she seemed frightened and unsure. But looking through the glass, I was convinced that with Maria Radovich, it was no act.

She jumped when I opened the door. "Oh! Mr. Goodwin?"

"The selfsame," I answered with a slight bow and an earnest smile. "And you are Maria Radovich, I presume? Please come in out of the twenty-percent chance of showers."

I hung her trenchcoat on the hall rack and motioned toward the office. Walking behind her, I could see that her figure, set off by a skirt of fashionable length, was a bit fuller than I remembered Mia Farrow's to be, and that was okay with me.

"Mr. Wolfe doesn't come down to the office for another hour and ten minutes," I said, motioning to the yellow chair nearest my desk. "Which is fine, because he wouldn't see you anyway. At least not right now. He thinks he's retired from the detective business. But I'm not." I flipped open my notebook and swiveled to face her.

"I'm sure if Mr. Wolfe knew about my uncle's trouble, he would want to do something right away," she said, twisting a scarf in her lap and leaning forward tensely.

"You don't know him, Miss Radovich. He can be immovable, irascible, and exasperating when he wants to, which is most of the time. I'm afraid you're stuck with me, at least for now. Maybe we can get Mr. Wolfe interested, later, but to do that, I've got to know everything. Like for starters, who is your uncle and why are you worried about him?"

"He is my great-uncle, really," she answered, still using only the front quarter of the chair cushion. "And he is very well-known. Milan Stevens. I am sure you have heard of him—he is music director, some people say conductor, of the New York Symphony."

Not wanting to look stupid or disappoint her, or both, I nodded. I've been to the symphony four or five times, always with Lily Rowan, and it was always her idea. Milan Stevens may have been the conductor one or more of those times, but I wouldn't take an oath on it. The name was only vaguely familiar.

"Mr. Goodwin, for the last two weeks, my uncle has been getting letters in the mail—awful, vile letters. I think someone may want to kill him, but he just throws the letters away. I am frightened. I am sure that—"

"How many letters have there been, Miss Radovich? Do you have any of them?"

She nodded and reached into the shoulder bag she had set on the floor. "Three so far, all the same." She handed the crumpled sheets over, along with their envelopes, and I spread them on my desk. Each was on six-by-nine-inch notepaper, plain white, the kind from an inexpensive tear-off pad. They were hand-printed, in all caps, with a black felt-tip pen. One read:

MAESTRO
QUIT THE PODIUM NOW! YOU ARE DOING DAMAGE TO A GREAT ORCHESTRA PUT DOWN THE BATON AND GET OUT IF YOU DON'T LEAVE ON YOUR OWN, YOU WILL BE REMOVED—PERMANENTLY!

In fact, all three weren't exactly alike. The wording differed, though only slightly. The "on your own" in the last sentence was missing from one note, and the first sentence didn't have an exclamation point in another. Maria had lightly penciled the numbers 1, 2, and 3 on the backs of each to indicate the order in which they were received. The envelopes were of a similar ordinary stock, each hand-printed to Milan Stevens at an address in the East Seventies. "His apartment?" I asked.

Maria nodded. "Yes, he and I have lived there since we came to this country, a little over two years ago."

"Miss Radovich, before we talk more about these notes, tell me about your uncle, and yourself. First, you said on the phone that he and Mr. Wolfe knew each other in Montenegro."

She eased back into the chair and nodded. "Yes, my uncle—his real name is Stefanovic, Milos Stefanovic. We are from Yugoslavia. I was born in Belgrade, but my uncle is a Montenegrin. That's a place on the Adriatic. But of course I don't have to tell you that—I'm sure you know all about it from Mr. Wolfe.

"My uncle's been a musician and conductor all over Europe—Italy, Austria, Germany. He was conducting in London last, before we came here. But long ago, he did some fighting in Montenegro. I know little of it, but I think he was involved in an independence movement. He doesn't like to talk about that at all, and he never mentioned Mr. Wolfe to me until one time when his picture was in the papers. It was something to do with a murder or a suicide—I think maybe your picture was there too?"

I nodded. That would have been when Orrie died. "What did your uncle say about Mr. Wolfe?"

"I gather they had lost touch over the years. But he didn't seem at all interested in getting in touch with Mr. Wolfe. At the time I said, 'How wonderful that such an old friend is right here. What a surprise! You'll call him, of course?' But Uncle Milos said no, that was part of the past. And I got the idea from the way he acted that they must have had some kind of difference. But that was so long ago!"

"If you sensed your uncle was unfriendly toward Mr. Wolfe, what made you call?"

"After he told me about knowing Mr. Wolfe back in

Montenegro, Uncle Milos kept looking at the picture in the paper and nodding his head. He said to me, 'He had the finest mind I have ever known. I wish I could say the same for his disposition.' "

I held back a smile. "But you got the impression that your uncle and Mr. Wolfe were close at one time?"

"Absolutely," Maria said. "Uncle Milos told me they had been through some great difficulty together. He even showed me this picture from an old scrapbook." She reached again into her bag and handed me a gray-toned photograph mounted on cardboard and ragged around the edges.

They certainly fit my conception of a band of guerrillas, although none looked to be out of his teens. There were nine in all, posed in front of a high stone wall, four kneeling in front and five standing behind them. Some were wearing long overcoats, others had on woolen shirts, and two wore what I think of as World War I helmets. I spotted Wolfe instantly, of course. He was second from the left in the back row, with his hands behind his back and a bandolier slung over one shoulder. His hair was darker then, and he weighed at least one hundred pounds less, but the face was remarkably similar to the one I had looked at across the dinner table last night. And his glare had the same intensity, coming at me from a faded picture, that it does in the office when he thinks I'm badgering him.

To Wolfe's right in the photo was Marko Vukcic, holding a rifle loosely at his side. "Which one's your uncle?" I asked Maria.

She leaned close enough so I could smell her perfume and pointed to one of the kneelers in front. He was dark-haired and intense like most of the others, but he appeared smaller than most of them. None of the nine, though, looked as if he were trying to win a congeniality contest. If they were as tough as they appeared, I'm glad I wasn't fighting against them.

"This picture was taken up in the mountains," Maria said. "Uncle Milos only showed it to me to point out Mr. Wolfe, but he wouldn't talk any more about the other men or what they were doing."

"Not going to a picnic," I said. "I'd like to hang onto this for a while. Now, what about you, Miss Radovich?

How does it happen you're living with a great-uncle?"

She told me about how her mother, a widow, had died when she was a child in Yugoslavia, and that Stefanovic, her mother's uncle, had legally adopted her. Divorced and without children, he was happy to have the companionship of a nine-year-old. Maria said he gave her all the love of a parent, albeit a strict one, taking her with him as he moved around Europe to increasingly better and more prestigious conducting jobs. At some time before moving to England, he had changed his name to Stevens—she couldn't remember exactly when. It was while they were living in London that he was picked as the new conductor, or music director if you prefer, of the New York Symphony. Maria, who by that time was twenty-three, made the move with him, and she was now a dancer with a small troupe in New York.

"Mr. Goodwin," she said, leaning forward and tensing again, "my uncle has worked hard all his life to get the kind of position and recognition he has today. Now somebody is trying to take it away from him." Her hand gripped my forearm.

"Why not just go to the police?" I asked with a shrug.

"I suggested that to Uncle Milos, and he became very angry. He said it would leak out to the newspapers and cause a scandal at the symphony, that the publicity would be harmful to him and the orchestra. He says these notes are from a crazy person, or maybe someone playing a prank. I was with him when he opened the first one, or I might not know about any of this. He read it and said something that means 'stupid' in Serbo-Croatian, then crumpled the note and threw it in the wastebasket. But he hardly spoke the rest of the evening.

"I waited until he left the room to get the note from the basket. It was then that I said we should call the police. He became upset and said it was probably a prankster, or maybe a season-ticket holder who didn't like the music the orchestra had been playing."

"How long until the next note?" I asked.

"I started watching the mail after that. Six days later, we got another envelope printed just like the first one. I didn't open it—I never open my uncle's mail. But again I found the crumpled note in the wastebasket next to his desk in the library. This time I didn't mention it to him, and he said nothing about it to me, but again he seemed distressed.

"The third note came yesterday, six days after the second, and again I found it in the wastebasket. Uncle Milos doesn't know that I've seen the last two notes, or that I've saved all three."

"Miss Radovich, does your uncle have any enemies you know of, anyone who would gain by his leaving the symphony?"

"The music director of a large orchestra always has his detractors." She took a deep breath. "There are always people who think it can be done better. Some are jealous, others just take pleasure in scoffing at talented people. My uncle does not discuss his work very much at home, but I do know, from him and from others, that he has opposition even within the orchestra. But notes like this, I can't believe—"

"*Someone* is writing them, Miss Radovich. I'd like to hear more about your uncle's opposition, but Mr. Wolfe will be down in just a few minutes, and it's best if you're not here when he comes in. He may get interested in your problem, but you'll have to let me be the one to try getting him interested."

For the third time, Maria dove into her bag. She fished out a wad of bills and thrust it at me. "There's five hundred dollars here," she said. "That is just for agreeing to try to find out who's writing the notes. I can pay another forty-five hundred dollars if you discover the person and get him to stop." Five grand was a long way below what Wolfe usually got as a fee, but I figured that for Maria Radovich, it was probably big bucks. I started to return the money, then I drew back and smiled.

"Fair enough," I said. "If I can get Nero Wolfe to move, we keep this. Otherwise, it goes back to you. Now we've got to get you out of here. You'll be hearing from me soon—one way or the other." I wrote her a receipt for the money, keeping a carbon, and hustled her out to the hall and on with her coat.

My watch said ten fifty-eight as she went down the steps to the street. I rushed back to the office, put the money and receipt in the safe, and arranged Wolfe's morning mail in a pile on his blotter. Included in the stack was one item the carrier hadn't delivered: a faded fifty-year-old photograph.

2

I just had time to get my paper in the typewriter and start on yesterday's dictation when I heard the elevator coming down from the plant rooms. "Good morning, Archie, did you sleep well?" he asked as he walked across to his desk, arranged a raceme of orchids in the vase, then settled his bulk into the only chair he likes and rang for beer.

"Yes sir," I answered, looking up. Despite his size, and we're talking about a seventh of a ton here, I've never gotten used to how efficient Wolfe is when he moves. Somehow, you keep thinking he's going to trip or do something clumsy when he goes around behind his desk, but he never does. Everything is smooth, even graceful— if you can use that word with someone so large. Then there are his clothes. Fat people get a rap for being sloppy, but not Nero Wolfe. Today, as usual, he was wearing a three-piece suit, this one a tan tweed, with a fresh yellow shirt and a brown silk tie with narrow yellow stripes. His wavy hair, still brown but with a healthy dose of gray mixed in, was carefully brushed. He'd never admit it to me or anybody else, but Nero Wolfe spent his share of time in front of the mirror every morning, and that included shaving with a straight razor, something I quit trying years ago when I got tired of the sight of my own blood.

I kept sneaking glances at Wolfe while he riffled through the stack of mail. The photograph was about half-way down, but he took his time getting there, stopping as I knew he would to peruse a seed catalog. I typed on.

"Archie!" It was a high-grade bellow, the first one he'd uncorked in months.

I looked up, feigning surprise.

"Where did this come from?" he asked, jabbing at the picture.

"What's that, sir?" I raised one eyebrow, which always gets him because he can't do it.

"You know very well. How did this get here? What envelope was it in?"

"Oh, *that.* Well, let me think . . . yes, of course, I almost forgot. It was brought by a young woman, nice-looking, too. She thought you might be interested in helping her with a problem."

Wolfe glowered, then leaned forward and studied the photograph. "They must all be dead by now . . . Two were killed by firing squads, one died in a foolhardy duel, another drowned in the Adriatic. And Marko . . ."

"They're not *all* dead," I put in. "You aren't, not locally anyway, although you've been putting on a good imitation for a couple of years. And there's at least one other living man in that picture."

Wolfe went back to the photograph, this time for more than a minute. "*Stefanovic.*" He pronounced it far differently than I would have. "I have no knowledge of his death."

"You win a case of salt-water taffy," I said. "Not only is he still breathing, but he lives right here in New York. And what's more, he's famous. Of course he's changed his name since you knew him."

Wolfe shot me another glower. His index finger was tracing circles on the arm of the chair, the only outward indication that he was furious. I knew more than he did about something and was forcing him to ask questions, which made it even worse.

"Archie, I have suffered your contumacy for longer than I care to think about." He pursed his lips. "Confound it, report!"

"Yes, sir," I said, maintaining a somber expression. Then I unloaded everything verbatim, from Maria's phone call to the money. When I got to the part about the three notes, I opened the safe and pulled them out, but he refused to give them a glance. During my whole report, he sat with his eyes closed, fingers interlaced on his center mound. He interrupted twice to ask questions. When I was through, he sat in silence, eyes still closed.

After about five minutes, I said, "Are you asleep, or just waiting for me to call in a portrait painter so he can capture your favorite pose?"

"Archie, shut up!" That made it two bellows in one day. I was trying to think up something smart to say that would bring on a third and set a record, but Fritz came in and announced lunch.

Wolfe has a rule, never broken, that business is not to be discussed during meals, and it had been an easy rule to keep for the last two years, since there wasn't any business. That day, though, my mind was on other things and I barely tasted Fritz's superb sweetbreads. Wolfe, however, consumed three helpings at his normal, unhurried pace, while holding forth on the reasons why third parties have been unsuccessful in American elections.

We finally went back to the office for coffee. During lunch, I decided I'd pushed Wolfe enough and would leave the next move to him. We sat in silence for several minutes, and I was beginning to revise my strategy when he got up and went to the bookshelf. He pulled down the big atlas, lugged it back to his desk, and opened it. He looked at a page, then turned back to the photograph, fingering it gently.

"Archie?" He drew in a bushel of air, then let it out slowly.

"Yes, sir?"

"You know Montenegro, at least superficially."

"Yes, sir."

"You also know—I have told you—that in my youth there, I was impetuous and headstrong, and that I sometimes showed a pronounced lack of judgment."

"So you have said."

"A half-century ago in Montenegro, Milos Stefanovic and I were relatively close friends, although I never shared his consuming interest in music. We fought together, along with Marko and others in the photograph, for a cause in which we strongly believed. On one occasion in Cetinje, Stefanovic saved my life. And then, for reasons that are now irrelevant, he and I parted, not without rancor. I haven't seen him since that time, and I probably haven't thought about him for twenty years, at least. I mention this by way of telling you that we are faced with an extraordinary circumstance."

"Yes, sir." Although Wolfe's upstairs horsepower is far greater than mine, I've been around long enough to know when he's rationalizing. I stifled a smile.

"I am duty-bound to see this woman." He spread his hands in what for him is a dramatic gesture of helplessness. "I have no choice. Tell her to be here at three o'clock. Also, it's been a long time since Mr. Cohen has joined us for dinner. Call and invite him for tonight. And tell him we will be serving that cognac he enjoys so much."

I was delighted, of course, that Wolfe had agreed to see Maria. But his wanting Lon Cohen to come for dinner was a bonus. Lon works for the *Gazette*, where he has an office two doors from the publisher's on the twentieth floor. He doesn't have a title I'm aware of, but I can't remember a major story in New York that he didn't know more about than ever appeared in the *Gazette*, or anyplace else, for that matter. Lon and I play in the same weekly poker game, but he only comes to dinner at Wolfe's a couple of times a year, and it's almost always when Wolfe wants information. This is all right with Lon, because he's gotten a fat file of exclusive stories from us through the years, not to mention some three-star meals.

As it turned out, Lon was available, although he wanted to know what was up. I told him he'd just have to wait, and that there was some Remisier to warm his tummy after dinner. He said for that he'd sell any state secrets he had lying around the office. And Maria could make it at three. "Does this mean Mr. Wolfe will take the case?" she asked over the phone breathlessly.

"Who knows?" I answered. "But at least he'll see you, and that alone is progress."

I went to the kitchen to tell Fritz there would be a guest for dinner. "Archie, things are happening today, I can tell. Is he going back to work?"

Fritz always fusses when Wolfe is in one of his periodic relapses. He acts like we're on the brink of bankruptcy at all times and thinks that if Wolfe isn't constantly performing feats of detection, there won't be enough money to pay his salary or, more important, the food bills. Needless to say, the last two years of inactivity by Wolfe had left Fritz with a permanently long puss, and I more than once caught him in the kitchen wringing his hands, looking heavenward, and muttering things in

French. "Archie, he needs to work," Fritz would say. "He enjoys his food more then. Work sharpens his appetite." I always replied that his appetite seemed plenty sharp to me, but he just shook his head mournfully.

This time, though, I delighted to report that prospects were improving. "Keep your carving knives crossed," I told him, "and say a prayer to Brillat-Savarin."

"I'll do more than that," he said. "Tonight, you and Mr. Wolfe and Mr. Cohen will have a dinner to remember." Whistling, he turned to his work, and I whistled a bit myself on the way back to the office.

MURDER MOST BRITISH!

BANTAM
SHOP-AT-HOME
C·A·T·A·L·O·G

Special Offer
Buy a Bantam Book
for only 50¢.

Now you can have an up-to-date listing of Bantam's hundreds of titles plus take advantage of our unique and exciting bonus book offer. A special offer which gives you the opportunity to purchase a Bantam book for only 50¢. Here's how!

By ordering any five books at the regular price per order, you can also choose any other single book listed (up to a $4.95 value) for just 50¢. Some restrictions do apply, but for further details why not send for Bantam's listing of titles today!

Just send us your name and address and we will send you a catalog!
